THE HIDDEN WORLD OF Changers

№.4: The Selkie Song

by H. K. Varian

Simon Spotlight

New York London Toronto Sydney New Delhi

437 1957

SIMON SPOTLIGHT
An imprint of Simon & Schuster Children's Publishing Division
1230 Avenue of the Americas, New York, New York 10020
This Simon Spotlight hardcover edition November 2016
Copyright © 2016 by Simon & Schuster, Inc.
Text by Ellie O'Ryan
Illustrations by Tony Foti
All rights reserved, including the right of reproduction in whole or in part in any form.
SIMON SPOTLIGHT and colophon are registered trademarks of Simon & Schuster, Inc.
For information about special discounts for bulk purchases, please contact Simon & Schuster Special Sales at 1-866-506-1949 or business@simonandschuster.com.
Designed by Nick Sciacca
The text of this book was set in Celestia Antiqua.
Manufactured in the United States of America 1016 FFG
10 9 8 7 6 5 4 3 2 1
ISBN 978-1-4814-6967-8 (hc)
ISBN 978-1-4814-6966-1 (pbk)
ISBN 978-1-4814-6968-5 (eBook)
Library of Congress Catalog Card Number 2015954652

Selkie

Originating from the shores of Ireland and Scotland, selkies are Changers who can transform into a seal with the help of their selkie cloaks. Selkies are born with their cloaks, and as they age, the cloak ages with them. As such, selkies usually feel an intense bond with their cloak and will protect it at all costs.

Though selkies cannot transform without their cloaks, they are still one of the most powerful kinds of Changers due to their innate connection to magic. Selkie magic is manifested through the selkie songs, which can control the tide, summon storms, enchant objects, and even destroy another being's magic.

Because selkie songs are sung in a magical language, they cannot be written down or otherwise captured. The only way for a selkie youngling to learn a song is to be taught directly by another selkie.

PROLOGUE

The *selkie* cloak shimmered in the early Saturday morning sun as it spilled across her father's lap.

Give it to me, Fiona Murphy thought, her eyes fixed on the cloak. *What if . . .*

Dad tries to take it away?

Or hide it?

Or even . . . destroy it?

How could Fiona live without her *selkie* cloak, the most important, most precious item she had ever possessed? It didn't look like much—velvety soft gray material with the faintest hint of a sheen—but to Fiona, that cloak was *everything*. It was the only way she could change into her other form—a *selkie*, or seal. As a *selkie*, Fiona had been born with her cloak, but for most of her life, she'd been without it, ever since someone had taken it from her as a baby. But once she had discovered her true nature and found her cloak, buried in a battered old chest in the sand, Fiona had sworn she would never be apart from it again.

Ever.

"Dad, I can explain what that is—" Fiona began.

Her voice broke off unexpectedly when her father looked up at last—a long, terrible moment when they did nothing more than stare at each other. The expression in his eyes made Fiona shrink inside herself; a heartbreaking combination of anguish, betrayal, and most of all—fear.

"I know exactly what this is," he replied.

As the words slipped from his lips, Fiona saw her father clutch her precious *selkie* cloak even tighter. He might as well have reached into her chest and taken hold of her heart, which seemed to skip a beat.

"Please," Fiona said, her hands reaching for the cloak.

But her dad didn't give it up. He couldn't even look at

her. "I have to ask," he began. "That time you were in the water, during the first week of school . . ."

Fiona's heart sank. *Here it comes,* she thought.

"Did you really fall in?"

A long silence followed. *Please,* Fiona thought. *Don't make me say it.*

"Or did you transform?"

"It was the first time," Fiona whispered, staring at the ground.

Dad's heavy sigh made her look up just in time to see him cover his eyes with his hand. She'd thought he would be mad at her. After all, Dad had just caught her in a bold-faced lie—but instead, Dad looked . . . well, *defeated.*

Fiona wasn't sure what to say next. The truth was, she'd lied because she *had* to—she'd made vows of secrecy about the very existence of Changers, people who had the ability to shape-shift into mythological animals. Fiona wasn't the only one; in fact, there were three other kids at Willow Cove Middle School alone who were Changers: Darren Smith, who could transform into a massive bird called an *impundulu*; Gabriella Rivera, a *nahual* who could change into a ferocious jaguar; and Mack Kimura, a fox Changer known as a *kitsune*. Mack's grandfather was one of the First Four, a council of elders who ruled over all the Changers in the world.

Over the last few months the Changers had been threatened by an evil warlock known as Auden Ironbound who was determined to seize power from the First Four and control the Changers. Fiona and her friends had already engaged in several battles with Auden and his followers, but the skirmishes were much more challenging for Fiona, who hadn't learned *selkie* magic yet. The other Changers didn't need a cloak or any sort of magical object to transform, either, which was just one reason why Fiona's *selkie* cloak was so vital, why she couldn't risk losing it. . . .

"Fiona, I'm going to ask you something else, and it's essential that you answer me honestly," Dad finally said. "Have you been contacted by another Changer? Perhaps another *selkie*? Or—or—"

Or what? Fiona wondered as Dad's voice faltered.

"Or your mother?"

Fiona blinked in surprise, unsure if she'd heard him

correctly. Mom had died when Fiona was three. But the very thought that there was a way, somehow, for Fiona to contact her again filled her with hope. *Can selkies communicate with the dead?* she wondered as her imagination ran wild. *Maybe that's one of their secret powers that can only be learned from another* selkie! *Maybe—*

Then Fiona's rational, whip-smart self caught up with her imagination. She had researched *selkies* constantly since she'd found out the truth about herself, and nowhere—*nowhere*—had there been even the slightest hint that *selkies* had such a power.

And since when did Dad, of all people, know about Changers and *selkies*?

Fiona chose her next words very carefully.

"Dad," she said slowly, "why did you ask if I'd seen Mom?"

This time, it was Dad's turn to be silent.

"Dad?" Fiona said again.

He sighed before answering at last. "Fiona, your mother is alive—and a *selkie*, like you."

Chapter 1
LEANA MURPHY

Fiona felt as though the world was suddenly very far away. The sound of the ocean outside her father's window disappeared, and everything went quiet as the truth hurtled through Fiona's mind.

Mom. Alive.

Then came the questions, hundreds of them, far too many for Fiona to process at once. She opened her mouth, but before she could speak, Dad placed his hand on her arm.

"I'm going to make some tea," he said.

"Tea?" Fiona repeated.

"I think we could both use a cup for the conversation we're about to have."

And then, just like that, Fiona was all alone. More alone than she'd been in weeks, actually; it didn't escape her notice that Dad had taken the *selkie* cloak with him. *What if he never gives it back?*

Then Fiona shook her head. *Don't think like that,* she scolded herself.

Fiona's gaze drifted to the stack of photos that Dad had been looking at when she'd burst into the room. They were everywhere: the bureau, the bedspread, the floor. Fiona knelt down to pick them up. There was Mom, reading a book to baby Fiona; there was Mom, laughing as Dad fed her a bite of cake at their wedding; there was Mom, sitting on Broad Rock, staring wistfully at the ocean.

That photo was enough to make Fiona sit down hard on the edge of the bed. Broad Rock was Fiona's favorite place to go when she wanted to be alone; it had been for as long as she could remember. How many times had Fiona sat there, just like Mom, staring out at the ocean with a longing that could never be put into words?

This is so much bigger than I ever imagined, Fiona realized. All the wondering and worrying that had consumed her since she first discovered her *selkie* cloak didn't even begin to scratch the surface.

Fiona stood up abruptly and neatly stacked the rest of the photos in an old shoebox. She had questions—so many questions! Now it was time to get some answers.

In the kitchen Dad was sitting at the table, waiting for her. His smile was crooked, as though he couldn't quite manage it, but was trying as hard as he could.

Like he always has, Fiona thought suddenly, thinking back on all the years that Dad had been like a father *and* a mother to her.

"Just how you like it," Dad said as he pushed a blue mug across the table. Fiona took a small sip. The tea had plenty of sugar and rich cream, and the warm comfort of it was exactly what she needed.

"The photos," Dad said, reaching for the box that Fiona had placed on the table between them. "I always figured the day would come when you'd want—need— to see them. Go ahead. Ask me anything. I promise I'll do my best to answer."

Fiona opened her mouth, then closed it, then opened it again. "I don't even know where to begin," she finally said.

"I understand," Dad told her. "Maybe I should just ... begin at the beginning."

Dad rummaged through the photos; when he found the one he was looking for, his whole face lit up. "Your mother and I met at the New Brighton Gaelic Traditions Festival," he said as he handed the photo to Fiona.

Fiona stared at the picture, which showed Mom standing at a microphone. Her red hair gleamed brightly in the sun from beneath a crown of blue wildflowers.

"I was still in graduate school back then," Dad continued. "Not many people cared about ancient Gaelic storytelling, but I was determined to change that. I'd started a small journal about local artists who celebrated world cultures. It was about as popular as my field of study—which is to say, not very popular at all." Dad chuckled at the memory.

"Anyway, I was wandering around the festival all by myself, when I paused at a tent that was dedicated to story-telling. And there was Leana—your mother—captivating the audience with her story about the lost *selkie* queen, Caileigh. I'd never been in love before—To be honest, I had started to think that maybe romantic love didn't even exist."

Fiona hid her smile; Dad was a professor, and sometimes it was all too easy for his logical side to take over. "And Mom changed your mind?" she asked.

"It was love at first sight," Dad confessed, a rueful smile on his face.

"Did Mom feel it too?"

"Amazingly, yes," Dad said. "It's as hard for me to believe now as it was then. The moment Leana finished her story, our eyes met, and that was it. We were inseparable." He held out another photo of them walking on the beach, arm in arm.

"I'd never known anyone like Leana before," Dad continued. "She was free, in every way—wild, almost. She followed her heart in all things. I found her inspirational. And somehow, your mother had fallen in love with me—someone her polar opposite, who was very much constrained by research and study. That was when I realized that my life wouldn't be complete without your mother in it. Perhaps her impulsive nature was rubbing off on me, but I proposed to her just months after we met."

"It sounds like a fairy tale," Fiona said.

"I suppose it was, in many ways," Dad replied. "It

certainly felt that way at the time. Unfortunately, though, Leana and I weren't destined to have a happy ending. Not the way we expected, anyway."

A feeling of dread crept over Fiona; she took another sip of her tea. "What happened?" she said. If she hadn't longed for answers for such a long time, she might never have had the courage to ask.

"A few months after we got married, I woke up in the middle of the night. To this day I don't know why, but I could feel, in my heart, that something was about to happen. I found Mom down at the beach," Dad said. "She was barefoot, trembling, as pale as the full moon reflecting off the water. And pacing back and forth, wearing a deep trench into the damp sand."

"What was wrong with her?" Fiona asked.

"Nothing was *wrong*," Dad said; it was clear he was choosing his words carefully. "Your mother had found out that she was pregnant with you, Fiona. And she knew exactly what that would mean—how everything was going to change."

"So it was my fault she left?" Fiona asked, her voice barely louder than a whisper.

"Absolutely not," Dad said at once. "No, Fiona. Not at all. Perhaps I wasn't entirely clear before. I had no idea that your mother was a *selkie* when we married."

Fiona's mouth dropped open in shock. "She didn't tell you?"

Dad shook his head. "I'm sure it sounds incredible," he replied. "But you have to understand, she'd been sworn to secrecy for her entire life, as I'm sure you have."

All Fiona could do was nod.

"But that changed as soon as Leana learned she was expecting a child," Dad explained. "She knew there was a chance that the baby would be a *selkie*, and so she could no longer conceal the truth about her identity. She told me everything—about *selkies*, about Changers, even about witches and warlocks—right there on the beach."

"Were you angry with her for keeping so many secrets?" Fiona asked.

"Angry?" asked Dad. "Not at all. I loved her. And besides, can you imagine devoting your life to studying myths and then learning that they were all true? That *selkies* were real? Their world would be my world, even if I could only ever exist on the edges of it."

A wide smile crossed Dad's face as he looked at Fiona. "And seven months later you were born, Fee, wrapped in your beautiful cloak. Your mother and I both knew exactly what that meant."

But Fiona knew that wasn't the end of the story—not yet, at least. "What happened next?" she asked. "Was Mom okay? Did she—"

"Everything was fine at first," Dad interrupted. "Better than fine, really. I'd thought Leana and I couldn't possibly be happier, but once you were born, our joy increased tenfold."

Fiona let herself smile, but only for a moment; her next question was already on the tip of her tongue. "How come it didn't last?" she asked.

"I've asked myself that question hundreds of times," Dad said. "And the truth, Fiona, is that I don't really know. I've been able to piece some of it together over the years, but there are things that only your mother knows. And she took that knowledge with her when she disappeared."

Disappeared—not died, Fiona thought. But she didn't say a word.

"One night, very late, when you were still just a toddler, there was a knock at the door," Dad continued. The words seemed hard for him to say. Fiona watched his face carefully, but he couldn't seem to meet her gaze. "There was a woman on the doorstep, drenched to the bone, tendrils of seaweed clinging to her bare feet."

"A *selkie*," Fiona said.

"Yes," Dad replied. "A messenger. She wouldn't speak to me. To be honest, her eyes were filled with disgust when I answered the door. She had come bearing a message for your mother: The *selkies* were splitting from the Changers to form a separate nation, to be governed under their own authority. She had one word for Leana before she left, as mysteriously as she'd arrived."

"What was it?" Fiona asked breathlessly.

"'Choose.'"

Fiona clutched her mug of tea, but it had grown cold. Of course there had been a choice to make, and it was very clear, wasn't it, how Mom had chosen?

But Fiona had to hear it. She had to hear Dad say it.

"Leana left that night," Dad continued. "She told me that the *selkies* needed her, that whatever happened next, she had a responsibility—a duty—to her kind. I didn't understand. Didn't she have a duty to her family, too? To her daughter? But she promised she would return, so I didn't try to stop her."

"Did she?" asked Fiona.

"In a way," Dad said. "The first week she was gone was unbearable. I couldn't imagine how you and I could possibly go on without her. But then, just as I had begun to despair, Leana came home."

"But she didn't stay," Fiona said.

"No," Dad replied. "She returned for one day. Looking back on it now, she had changed, though I was too foolish, too in love to see it. Leana had already made her choice, I think. She came back not for good . . . but for good-bye."

Dad rested his hand on Fiona's *selkie* cloak. "That was when she hid this," he explained. "I wasn't sure I'd ever see it again. For some reason, Fiona, it was exceedingly important to her that you *not* have your *selkie* cloak, that you not know the truth about yourself."

"How come?" asked Fiona.

"That's another secret she took with her," Dad said. "I begged her for answers. For the truth. And above all, for her to stay. But she wouldn't. Sometimes, when I think about it, I wonder if it was really a choice, after all."

"And you never saw her again?" asked Fiona.

"Not exactly," Dad said. "Nine years have passed, but I still think I see her from time to time—but only in her seal form. She's quite lovely, you know, with a copper-colored pelt that gleams in the sunlight."

"The copper-colored seal!" Fiona gasped. "I've seen her!"

Dad's whole face broke into a smile. "I'm glad to hear that," he said. "I always had a feeling that she checks in on us."

"But . . . if you knew she was out there, if you *knew* she was coming around, why did you tell me she died?" asked Fiona.

"Because she asked me to," Dad replied. "Leana said that when you were old enough, she would explain everything. Perhaps I should've waited for her to come back, to let her tell you all this. But to be honest, I feel like I waited too long to speak up. It wouldn't be right to keep the truth from you any longer.

"If you want to find your mother, Fiona, I won't stop

you," Dad continued. "I wouldn't even try. And she must be close, for both of us to have seen her in the ocean. There is one thing I'd ask of you, though."

"What's that?"

"Be sure you're ready," Dad told her. "I can't prepare you for what Leana might be like now—or how it might feel to see her again after all these years. Only you will know if you're prepared."

With that, Dad placed the *selkie* cloak in Fiona's lap.

And she burst into tears.

Dad wrapped his arms around Fiona. "You must feel like your whole world's been turned upside down. But I know you can get through this, Fiona. You're strong."

Fiona buried her face in her dad's shoulder. A strange mix of emotions was fighting inside her. She cried for her brokenhearted father, who had worked so hard to raise her all these lonely years. She cried thinking of the things her mother had missed, moments that the two of them would never get back.

But more than anything, Fiona cried from joy, from relief, from *glee*—Mom was alive! Every time Fiona had longed to see her, Mom had been just out in the ocean, keeping a watchful eye. The questions that had consumed Fiona no longer seemed so impossible to answer. In fact, the answers she needed now seemed closer than ever.

Just like Mom herself.

The shift in Fiona's emotions was sudden. *She's been close this whole time,* she thought. *What—what was she waiting for?*

Didn't she know that Fiona missed her? Didn't she know that Fiona needed her?

Didn't she know that Fiona was twelve years old now, and facing all the marvelous, terrifying realities of being a Changer?

Fiona forced herself to stop crying and took a deep, shuddering breath. She looked up, over Dad's shoulder, toward the kitchen window, where she could see the ocean glittering under the morning sun. There was still one question, Fiona realized, that was troubling her more than all the others.

Mom, she thought. *Why did you leave us?*

Chapter 2
THE CHOICE

Gabriella sat cross-legged on the bed, her phone perched precariously on her knee as she dried her long, thick hair. Normally, Gabriella wasn't one of those people who was totally obsessed with her phone every moment, but Fiona's text—all caps, with more exclamation marks than Gabriella had ever seen in her life—told her that the situation was urgent. Gabriella hadn't wasted a moment canceling her usual Saturday morning practice with Tía Rosa, who was teaching Gabriella how to control her *nahual* powers.

Not too long ago, Gabriella had been on the brink of despair, certain that she was at risk of transforming into a jaguar when she least expected it. Thankfully, Gabriella had discovered that her favorite aunt wasn't just a *nahual*—Tía Rosa was also the Emerald Wildcat, a real-life Changer superhero who had thwarted crimes in the nearby city of New Brighton. Tía Rosa had promised Gabriella that in time, she would be able to control her powers just as skillfully. At first, it was hard to believe, but after a few sessions with her aunt, Gabriella had started to suspect that Tía Rosa might be right.

Gabriella's hair was still a little damp when the text she'd been waiting for finally arrived.

I'm here.

Gabriella shoved her phone into her pocket and zipped downstairs to let Fiona in. Fiona's pale face looked even whiter than usual, making her freckles pop like bright sparks.

"Come in and tell me *everything*," Gabriella said as she led Fiona to the kitchen. "Ma and Maritza are out for the day. They won't be back until dinnertime. I told Tía Rosa I couldn't do training today, but if you think we need her help . . ."

"No . . . not yet, anyway," Fiona replied. Her eyes

grew wide as she looked around the kitchen. "Wow! Everything is fixed. It looks amazing in here! You'd never know that the room was completely destroyed."

"I know, right?" Gabriella exclaimed. "Ma always wanted a fancy new kitchen. . . . Too bad she'll never know she has a pack of warlocks to thank for it!"

The truth was, the attack from the warlocks over Circe's Compass, a powerful magical object that could be used to find any Changer in the world, had been seriously scary—but sometimes it helped to laugh about the Changers' crazy exploits.

"So . . . what's up? Your texts had me worried," Gabriella said. Fiona followed Gabriella upstairs to her room, where the hair dryer was still lying on the floor. "Sorry," Gabriella said as she kicked it under the bed, along with a pile of dirty clothes. "I'm kind of a slob."

"You're fine," Fiona said in an absentminded way as she perched on the end of the bed.

There was an awkward silence.

"It's okay," Gabriella finally said. She wasn't sure if it was the right thing to say, but it felt right. "Whatever's going on, you can trust me."

"I know," Fiona said quickly. "It's just— I don't really know where to begin. My dad found my *selkie* cloak."

"He *what*?!" Gabriella cried. "Is he going to stop you from coming to Changers class? Is he—"

"No, no. And really, that's not the crazy part."

Gabriella gave Fiona a skeptical look. She wasn't sure what could top Fiona's dad finding out that she was a magical shape-shifter.

"He told me that my mom is still alive. And . . . she's a *selkie* too."

"What?!" Gabriella exclaimed, louder than she meant. "I mean, *what*?"

"Exactly!" Fiona said, throwing her arms into the air and flopping backward onto the bed. Suddenly, she wasn't at a loss for words anymore—the story spilled out of her almost faster than Gabriella could keep up. As Fiona came to the end of her story, Gabriella whistled low.

"And you mean to tell me that the *selkies* were trying to *split off from the Changers*?" Gabriella asked incredulously. "Is that even possible?"

Fiona shrugged. "I'm not sure. After my mom disappeared, my dad didn't get any more information," she replied. "But my guess is that they did separate. After all, it would explain why I haven't been able to find a *selkie* to mentor me—and why even the First Four can't help."

"I can't believe it," Gabriella said. "It's so sad. I mean, Changers should *always* stick together."

"I'm sure they had their reasons," Fiona said. There was an unexpected edge to her voice that made Gabriella take a closer look at her friend.

"So . . . what are you going to do?" Gabriella asked carefully. "Do you think you'll try to find your mom?"

"I . . . don't know," Fiona replied. "Even up until an hour ago, I thought my answer would be an automatic *yes*. But . . . how come my mom never came back for me? Why did she let me struggle without having a mom for so long? With being a *selkie* all by myself?"

This time, there was nothing Gabriella could say to fill the weighty silence. Gabriella's dad had left her family when she was younger, too. She knew what it was like to deal with that kind of empty feeling.

"But she's been watching over me," Fiona continued, as if she were trying to convince herself. "And I need her to help me unlock the *selkie* songs—and my powers. I've been so useless."

"Stop that—" Gabriella began, but Fiona cut her off.

"Of course I've been useless," she said. "There's no other word for it. Like when we were trying to save Darren from Auden's henchman, Jasper. All I could do was stay out of the way. Maybe if I'd been able to access the *selkie* songs . . . Jasper wouldn't have escaped with the Horn of Power."

"Seriously, don't talk like that," Gabriella said firmly. "I've done that to myself before, and there's no way to know how things could've been different. You just need a little extra help—we all do."

Fiona tried to smile, but Gabriella could tell she wasn't fully convinced.

"Trust me on this," Gabriella added. "You remember what I was like before Tía Rosa started training me. I was a total disaster."

Fiona opened her mouth in protest, but Gabriella stopped her. "But now, every week, I feel like my powers are getting easier to manage. And my transformations are almost completely under control! I know it'll be the same for you, as soon as you have a *selkie* to guide you. And I can't *wait* to see what your powers are like once you've unlocked them."

This time, Fiona's smile wasn't a bit forced. "Thanks." She paused, looking for the right words to say. "I know it sounds really cheesy, but I'm glad we're friends."

Gabriella blushed. She had to admit, she was glad to have Fiona as a friend, too. Before she'd found out she was a Changer, Gabriella had been one of the most popular girls in school, but it came at a cost. Gabriella could never really be herself; she always had to tease other kids or put herself down when she was with her popular friends. But these last few months, being a Changer with Fiona and Darren and Mack, she felt . . . free.

"It seems like a million years ago that I was hanging out with Lizbeth Harris and her dumb clique," Gabriella said, making a face. "I have no idea what I was thinking. . . . I hated being mean like them."

"You weren't mean," Fiona assured her. "Back then, I just figured that someone like *you* would never want to be friends with someone like *me*. You've always been so cool and strong."

"Why wouldn't I want to be friends with you, Fiona? You're smart and interesting, and, well, nice. Which is more than I can say of Lizbeth." Gabriella laughed.

Fiona was about to respond when the front door suddenly banged open.

"Gabriella! *Mija!* Where is your sweet self?" a voice called out from downstairs.

"It's Tía Rosa," Gabriella said to Fiona. She crossed the room and poked her head out the doorway. "*Buenos dias*, Tía Rosa!" she replied. "Didn't you get my text?"

"I was halfway here already, so I decided to come, anyway," Tía Rosa replied. She appeared at the base of the stairs and beamed up at Gabriella and Fiona. "Girls' day! How fun! Why don't you come down and I'll fix you some *xocolatl*?"

"Awesome! We'll be right there," Gabriella replied.

"What's *xocolatl*?" asked Fiona.

A sly smile crossed Gabriella's face. "You'll see," she said mysteriously. "All I can tell you is that it's a drink for Aztec warriors, from an old family recipe."

A few minutes later the girls joined Tía Rosa in the kitchen as she ladled the steaming *xocolatl* into three mugs.

"Oh! It's hot chocolate!" Fiona exclaimed as she took her mug. "I love cocoa."

"Then you'll love this," Gabriella told her.

Fiona took a big gulp, and her pale face was suddenly flooded with color. "Spicy! So spicy!" she gasped, waving her hand in front of her mouth. Gabriella and Tía Rosa couldn't help laughing.

"Don't worry, you'll get used to it," Gabriella said with a wink. She hopped off her stool and moved over to the sink to get Fiona a glass of water. "You *are* a warrior, even if—"

There came a sudden piercing shriek, so loud and sharp that Gabriella didn't even notice when the glass slipped from her hand and shattered onto the floor. Everything around her faded to black. She stumbled, grasping for the counter, but there was nothing, nothing, nothing but that shriek. . . .

And then a silence that brought her to her knees, followed by a deep voice.

My brethren, I have returned to you.

Chapter 3
THE RETURN

It is I, Auden Ironbound. I come to you now, revitalized, ready to usher in a new world order. No longer will non-magical beings rule over their betters. The time has come for Changers and magic to unite to create one supreme people; to declare an end to non-magical dominance by any means necessary.

For too long we have been confused, my brothers and sisters. We have been fighting the wrong enemy. We have been fighting one another instead of our true foe. And so I invite all magical beings to join me at dawn on the beach of Willow Cove in two days' time. The corrupt reign of the First Four will come to a glorious end as we usher in a new age. Join me. Join us.

And if you don't, you will regret your error. For I have the Horn of Power now, fully restored and ready to exert control over each and every individual who resists. Those who try to stand alone will fall together.

The time has come. The time is now.

Join me.

The voice faded from Mack's mind; in stages the regular world returned to him: first light, then color, then sound. A sickening feeling of dread washed over Mack. "Jiichan," he whispered to his grandfather, who was sitting, motionless, at the table.

Jiichan did not respond.

What if Auden Ironbound has cursed him? Mack worried.

But a closer look at Jiichan's face, which appeared even more calm and peaceful than usual, helped Mack realize what was really going on. His grandfather, after all, was over a thousand years old, and perhaps the most powerful Changer of all time. As a nine-tailed *kitsune*, Jiichan had the ability to slip into a deep, meditative trance and locate any Changer or magic-user in the world—as long as they weren't shrouded by enchantments.

Maybe Jiichan can find Auden Ironbound and put an end to this before it starts, Mack thought hopefully. Mack had already faced Auden Ironbound once before. He would never forget their battle on the beach as an army of Changers, hypnotized by the Horn of Power, bore down on Willow Cove. By drawing on all of their powers, Mack had been able to damage the Horn of Power and delay Auden Ironbound's plans for conquest—but not for long. The warlock had gone to great and terrible lengths to repair the horn, even kidnapping Darren and four other young Changers. Now, Mack suspected, Auden would be even more determined to succeed.

Mack reached for his cell phone and sent a group text to Fiona, Gabriella, and Darren.

> Did you hear that?

Their responses came flooding in.

> Darren Smith **Yeah. Glad it wasn't just me.**

> Gabriella Rivera **I heard it too. So he's back?**

> Fiona Murphy **Me too. What does your grandfather say, Mack?**

Mack glanced up from his phone to see that Jiichan, no longer meditating, was watching him.

"Tell your friends to meet us at the gymnasium," Jiichan said in an even voice. "There is no time to lose."

When Mack and Jiichan arrived at the ancillary gym at school a few minutes later, everyone else was already there—not just Fiona, Gabriella, and Darren, but the rest of the First Four too: Yara Moreno, Sefu Badawi, and the kids' independent study teacher, Ms. Dorina Therian. Yara and Sefu had their heads bent, deep in a private conversation, but Ms. Therian's fury bubbled right under the surface of her steely exterior.

"A clever trick!" she raged, approaching Jiichan so swiftly that her long braid swung back and forth behind her. "If we go to the beach, Auden Ironbound will turn us on the younglings, just like last time. If we don't go, we're seen as cowards to our kind, hiding behind children. He won't need to depose us; we would never be able to lead our people again!"

"There is but one thing to do," Sefu announced gravely. "We must leave Willow Cove at once, go into hiding until we can come up with our own plan of attack."

"You're both blind," came Yara's voice. Everyone turned to look at her, but Yara was staring at Fiona, as if no one else was in the room. "Don't you see? There is another way to prevent Auden's rise, and it's standing right in front of us."

"Absolutely not," Jiichan spoke for the first time since he had arrived.

"But—" Yara began.

"You know the treaty," Jiichan said sternly. "You know who leads them. Would you have our entire arrangement crumble? Make no mistake, our peace is a fragile one. A single wrong move could bring us to the brink of war. No, Yara. We will find another way."

Mack had no idea what Yara and Jiichan were arguing about, but in the silence that followed, he felt compelled to speak up. "Um, this might be a stupid question, but can't I just face Auden Ironbound on the beach like last time?" he asked. "I was totally inexperienced back then, but I still beat him. I've learned *so* much since then. I know I could take him again."

A troubled look settled over Jiichan's lined face. "Makoto, we all admire your courage," he began, "but no, I am afraid it would be unwise to assume you could re-create your triumph. Auden Ironbound is deviously clever. He would not invite a repeat performance of his last defeat unless he was certain he would prevail."

Mack sighed. He hated to admit it, but he knew Jiichan was probably right. Before he could respond, though, Jiichan continued. "I would like to see how far you've all progressed in your training."

Mack cracked a smile for about half a second before he changed into his *kitsune* form. He wasn't the only one, either; there was a flurry of activity in the ancillary gym—

A gust of wind ruffled Mack's fur as Darren transformed into an *impundulu* and beat his powerful, blue-feathered wings.

In her *nahual* form, Gabriella inched forward on inky black paws. Her golden eyes sparkled with determination.

And Fiona?

A single spin, her *selkie* cloak fluttering as she wrapped it across her shoulders, and Fiona was a seal.

Sefu stepped forward. A thick mist rose from the

ground at his feet, spiraling upward until it formed a cloud over his head. Just as suddenly as it had formed, the cloud dissolved, pelting Sefu with raindrops that sizzled as they hit his ancient skin. When they were gone, a spotted hyena—a *bultungin*—stood in Sefu's place.

The hyena growled—a low, threatening sound— and Mack understood right away that Sefu, their mentor, their guide, was going to fight them. Sefu's fur bristled as he bared his sharp teeth.

Mack was poised to attack when, to his surprise, Darren swooped in front of him. The great bird lifted his talons, which crackled with electrical current. Mack watched, awestruck, as Darren's talons began to spark; then the sparks joined forces, forging a glowing web of electricity. Darren's force field crackled, an unmistakable warning.

Sefu paced around the force field, growling. After three full loops he was finally satisfied that the force field was impenetrable; there wasn't a single opening that he could find. Just in time, too. Mere moments after Sefu stepped back, Darren landed, transformed, and collapsed to the ground.

Mack lunged toward his friend.

He's fine, Makoto, Jiichan's voice rang through Mack's head. *Creating a force field like that is very tiring. He'll feel better after a short rest.*

Mack nodded in response as Sefu approached. His turn had come.

He felt the heat rising from his paws before the thought had even fully formed in his mind: *fireballs.* It was a skill he'd been practicing in private—Mack didn't want anyone to see him fail again and again while he tried to get it right.

Mack's copper fur blazed as yellow flames licked at his paws. He crouched forward, his head bowed low, almost as though he were about to pounce, and concentrated on building the flame. *Patience . . . patience . . . ,* Mack counseled himself. Too many times he'd tried to throw a fireball before it was ready—only to watch it fizzle out into a puff of useless smoke.

This time, though, Mack's self-control paid off. A ring of perfectly formed fireballs appeared in a circle around him, white-hot flames leaping into the air. His eyes never left Sefu as Mack took aim and hurled each fiery orb directly at one of the greatest Changers in the world. The *last* thing Mack wanted to do was hit Sefu, but he knew that the First Four expected nothing less than his best effort—no matter what the risk.

Despite his advanced age (Sefu was, after all, just as old as Jiichan), Sefu leaped nimbly out of each fireball's path. From the sidelines, Jiichan quickly cast enchantments to destroy the fireballs in midair. They fizzled out even as Mack prepared to launch another round at Sefu. Again and again, Sefu skillfully dodged each one until, at last, he nodded respectfully at Mack— then turned toward Gabriella.

Mack's forelegs were trembling from the exertion of creating so much fire, but he didn't feel disappointed at not hitting Sefu. Even thought Sefu had dodged every attack, Mack had proven himself against one of the First Four, and that was no small thing.

Sefu approached Gabriella next, but she was ready for him. Her agility was uncanny as she feinted, dodging his every attack, almost anticipating Sefu's next move before he even made it. Mack realized that Gabriella wasn't just avoiding Sefu.

She was exhausting him.

That's awesome, Mack thought. Her defenses were so sophisticated that she never even had to swipe at Sefu. Before long, Sefu bowed to Gabriella. Her trial was over.

Now only Fiona was left.

Mack tilted his head, watching with interest as Sefu approached Fiona. *How will Fiona defend herself from a land Changer's attack?* he wondered. It was no secret that Fiona couldn't really use her *selkie* abilities on land.

Mack wasn't in suspense for long. Fiona let the *selkie* cloak fall from her shoulders, causing an immediate transformation back to her human form.

"I won't fight you," she said. "What would be the point?"

The air crackled with tension as everyone waited for Sefu to respond. He stared at Fiona, giving no indication to his thoughts.

"I'm useless," she continued. "I can't defend myself on land—not without the *selkie* songs."

Sefu transformed then, but still didn't speak. Fiona turned to face Ms. Therian.

"I want to find my mother," she said. "I'm ready to learn the songs."

One, two, three: Mack, then Darren, and finally Gabriella transformed, all in fast succession. Mack shot a glance at Darren, who looked as baffled as Mack felt.

Fiona's mom is dead—right? Mack asked Darren telepathically.

That's what I thought, Darren replied.

But how come none of the First Four looked surprised by Fiona's request?

Or Gabriella, for that matter?

"Fiona," Yara began.

Ms. Therian held up a hand to stop her. But Yara would not be silenced.

"She has a right to know," Yara continued, with an urgency in her voice that Mack had never heard before. "Fiona. Your mother isn't just another *selkie.* She's their queen."

Chapter 4
FIONA'S MISSION

Darren's face scrunched up in disbelief. *What* was going on? Had Yara really announced that Fiona's mother wasn't just alive, but that she was the queen of the *selkies*? *How can selkies even have a queen?* he wondered. The First Four were the leaders of all the Changers. Everyone knew that.

"She's their *queen*?" Fiona gasped. "My father . . . He told me—he told me that the *selkies* split from the Changers—"

"Yes," Mr. Kimura said, nodding his head. "That is correct."

"So they're not really under the rule of the First Four?" continued Fiona.

"No, they're not," Yara confirmed. "The *selkies* are a sovereign nation unto themselves. They answer to no one—no one but their queen."

Fiona's hands fluttered toward her temples. "How did this *happen?*" she asked.

"Yeah," Mack spoke up. "What you've told us . . . You've always said that the Changers have to be united. Strength in numbers. But you just let the *selkies* abandon everyone else?"

"Hey—that's not fair," Fiona said, frowning. "They didn't abandon anyone!"

Yara held up both her hands. "This is a very complicated chapter in Changers history," she said. "But rest assured, you will learn all about it in the course of your training. What matters now is that Fiona's mother, as queen of *selkie*-kind, is the keeper of a powerful song that can stop, and, if sung under ideal circumstances, even strip away one's magic. It is one of the most effective weapons available to Changers."

A song as a weapon? Darren thought. How could something as innocent as music be considered a weapon? Then again, Darren realized, he'd never actually seen *selkie* magic in action. Darren glanced over at Fiona and wondered, for the first time, exactly *what* she would be capable of achieving once her powers were unlocked.

"Rather, it *was* available to Changers," Ms. Therian quickly corrected Yara. "Since the severing of our nations, we have not had access to this song."

"This time is different!" Yara argued. "We have an emissary—an ambassador—someone to bridge the gap between our worlds! If Fiona can reach her mother, if she can convince the *selkies* to fight with us, her mother can seize the magic of Auden Ironbound and his entire army."

"And the Changers would have a fighting chance," added Sefu.

"Why does it have to be Fiona?" Gabriella spoke up protectively. "Wouldn't it be better if the First Four talked to the *selkie* queen? After all, Auden Ironbound is a threat to *selkies*, too, isn't he?"

"For many years we have existed under a fragile peace," Mr. Kimura explained. "The terms of our treaty specifically state that only *selkies*—and no other Changer—are allowed to enter their territory. That includes, of course, the islands off the coast, where we believe Queen Leana resides."

"The Isles of Saorsie," Sefu spoke up.

Mr. Kimura turned to Fiona. "That is why we cannot approach the *selkies*, but *you* can," he explained. "You are the only one who has the right to pass through those waters. Sending anyone else would be a declaration of war."

"Of course I'll go," Fiona said.

Ms. Therian shook her head. "You don't have to decide on the spot," she said. "We're asking a great deal of you, Fiona. You haven't even seen your mother for nine years."

"It doesn't matter," Fiona replied. "It's the only way we can stop Auden. Besides, I—"

For a moment Fiona faltered. When she spoke again, though, her voice was stronger than ever. "I need to find my mother. She's been gone for so long, and I have so many questions. I have to know why she left—I have to know the *selkie* songs—I have to *know*—"

Gabriella crossed the room so quickly that Darren thought she had to have used her *nahual* speed. "Are you sure?" she asked, locking eyes with Fiona. "Are you sure you want to do this?"

Fiona nodded. "More sure than I've ever been about anything," she replied.

"You must make the journey alone, as soon as possible," Ms. Therian told her. "Tomorrow at dawn, I think; it will be a swim of several hours, and you must seize the light while you can."

No, Darren thought suddenly. *This is nuts. It's too dangerous.* He remembered all too well what had happened when his desire to master his powers had gotten the better of him, making him vulnerable to a sneak attack that helped Auden Ironbound's underling Jasper repair the Horn of Power. It was clear that Fiona was just as desperate to unlock her *selkie* powers—but was anyone else thinking about the risk involved?

"Hang on a minute," Darren spoke up. "Are you *sure* this is the only way?"

Everyone stared at him, but Darren pushed on.

"Am I the only one who thinks this is a bad idea?" he asked. "You're just going to, like, send Fiona out to who-knows-where in the middle of the ocean, searching for her mom who, may I remind you, faked her own death?"

Fiona shook her head. "It's more complicated than that," she said.

"Yeah, sure, I have no doubt," Darren replied. "But . . . I'm *worried* about you. You haven't seen your mom in years. Do you even remember her?"

Then he spun around to face the First Four. "What do you know about her mother? Have you even spoken to her since the split? What if she, like, kidnaps Fiona and keeps her with the *selkies*? Did you think about that?"

"That's enough," Yara said sharply. "We never said this plan was without risk. But it is still Fiona's decision to make."

Darren was quiet, but the answer didn't satisfy him. For the first time he felt a little uneasy about the First Four's intentions. Desperate times called for desperate measures, but to risk Fiona's safety . . .

I'll be okay. Fiona's voice rang through his head. Darren looked up at her, and she met his gaze. *There are things about my mom I haven't told you and Mack yet. I'll explain later.*

"We have been formulating an alternate plan," Sefu spoke up, breaking Darren's concentration. "But right now, it is even riskier, and more likely to fail, unless we can figure out a way to—"

"We should continue those discussions at once," Mr. Kimura spoke up suddenly. "No doubt great numbers of Changers will descend upon Willow Cove soon. We must prepare for their arrival. I believe we have seen what we need to see from your students, Dorina. You should be very proud of their progress—and so should they."

"Can Darren, Gabriella, and Fiona come over to our house?" asked Mack.

Mr. Kimura nodded slowly. "Of course," he said. "It would do us all well to remember that in these dark times, the light of friendship burns brightest."

Back at Mack's house, the First Four disappeared into Mr. Kimura's study, closing the door firmly behind them. Gabriella stared at the door's intricate latticework and translucent rice-paper panels. "Wish we could hear what they're saying," she said wistfully.

"Not a chance," Mack said. "I always used to wonder why I couldn't hear through the panels. I mean, they're literally paper. That's made of rice."

"But it's enchanted, right?" Fiona said with a knowing look.

"Must be," Mack confirmed. "I'm sure Jiichan has some kind of magic protecting his entire study."

Fiona rubbed her temples. "This day," she began. "I can't even."

"What happened this morning?" Darren asked her. "That news about your mom . . . You must be reeling."

"It's like a crazy dream," Fiona said. "I keep expecting to wake up and realize that none of this is actually happening."

"You should tell them," Gabriella spoke up, nodding toward Mack and Darren. "What you told me, I mean."

"Only if you want to," Darren said quickly.

"Of course I do," Fiona said. Then she launched into the whole story of her dad finding the cloak, and the tale he'd told her. When she finished, Mack shook his head in astonishment.

"That's intense," he said. "Your mom really is alive,

huh? And you've been seeing her in the ocean! Can you believe how close she is?"

"No," Fiona said simply. "It's— It doesn't seem real."

"Does this make you a princess?" Mack blurted. "Fiona! You're royalty!"

A pink flush crept into Fiona's cheeks. "Who knows?" she said. "Maybe queen is just a title, like president."

"You think *selkies* have elections?" Darren asked. He meant it as a joke, but Fiona seriously considered it.

"I have no idea," she repeated. "I hardly know anything about my kind."

Something in her voice made Darren melancholic. True, Darren had been able to find more information on *impundulus* than Fiona had on *selkies*, but still . . . Having never met another *impundulu*, Darren often felt sort of . . . lonely. *Will I meet a Changer like me soon?* he thought. *Will I ever have a teacher or a friend or someone who truly understands what these powers are like?*

"It's sort of scary, to be honest," Fiona continued. "I have *no* idea what to expect. And no way to find out."

"Hang on," Darren said. "What about *The Compendium*? Maybe there's something—something we missed before, because we didn't know that the *selkies* had left the Changers. It's worth a try."

"But the First Four took it back, remember?" Fiona asked. "Who knows where it—"

Mack jumped up from the couch. "Jiichan has *The Compendium* in his study!" he exclaimed. Then he charged across the room and knocked loudly on the door.

The door opened a crack, just enough for Mr. Kimura's wrinkled face to appear. "Yes?" he asked.

"Can we borrow *The Compendium*?" asked Mack. "We were thinking Fiona could read it before her mission."

A small smile flickered across Jiichan's face. "Yes, of course," he said. He slipped back into the study for a moment and then reappeared with the ancient book, filled with thousands of years of knowledge about Changers. "Fiona, you may borrow this for the night. Please bring it with you to the beach tomorrow so you can return it to Ms. Therian before your journey."

"I will," Fiona said gratefully. "Thank you."

Darren watched as Mack placed the heavy book in Fiona's outstretched hands. "Books have always helped me get through tough stuff before," she said. "Let's hope

The *Compendium* doesn't fail me now. Thanks, Darren."

"It's nothing," he said. "I wish there was something more we could do."

"Me too," added Mack. "Your first solo mission . . ."

"You have to text us the minute you get back to the beach tomorrow night," Gabriella told Fiona. "Seriously, I'll be going crazy until I hear from you."

"Of course I will, but I'm sure it's not going to be that big of a deal," Fiona said. "I might not even find the *selkies'* islands. Or my mom. Besides, you'll be just fine without me. It's not like I've been able to help out much, anyway."

"What are you talking about?" Darren asked incredulously. "Without you, we never would've found *The Compendium* to begin with. Or learned that the Horn of Power can't affect younglings. Or discovered Circe's Compass in that shipwreck."

Fiona smiled but waved away the praise with a flick of her wrist. "I know you're trying to make me feel better, but the truth is, I've been deadweight during our battles—especially lately. I can barely defend myself on land, let alone fight alongside you. Sooner or later, it's going to happen: I'll drag us all down."

"Cut it out," Gabriella said firmly. "Tomorrow you're going to find the *selkies*—find your mom!—and start learning the *selkie* songs. *Tomorrow*. And after that, everything changes. Forever."

"Does it, though?" Fiona asked. Her eyes looked sad, but her voice sounded as practical as always. "Who really knows what the *selkie* songs can do? Or how long it takes to learn them? It could take years—decades, even—before I can master my powers."

"A journey of a thousand miles begins with a single step," Mack said suddenly.

"Huh?" asked Darren.

"Sorry," Mack replied. "I was just trying to channel Jiichan. He says stuff like that all the time. And you know what? I don't think he's wrong. I thought I'd *never* figure out how to transform, but once it happened, *everything* opened up for me. It will be the same for you, Fiona. I know it will. And so does Jiichan. Otherwise he wouldn't even let you go on this mission."

Fiona managed a smile. "I hope you're right," she replied.

But she didn't sound convinced.

Chapter 5
DACHAIGH

Dinner at Fiona's house was unusually subdued that night; Fiona had way too much on her mind to keep up a conversation. Luckily, Dad seemed to understand, for which Fiona was incredibly grateful.

"You can talk to me any time, Fee," he said near the end of their meal. "I want to make sure you know that."

"I do," she replied. "Thanks, Dad."

But the truth was, Fiona already sensed that there were things she would never, ever be able to tell him. After all, Dad was a regular human, and though he understood a whole lot more about Changers than most normal people, Fiona knew that keeping the Changers' secrets was necessary for everyone's safety. *How did Mom do it?* she wondered as her gaze drifted, like always, to the ocean view through the kitchen window. *How did she figure out what she could tell Dad . . . and what she needed to keep secret?*

Fiona couldn't help it; she sighed heavily. *Just more questions to add to my list, I guess,* she thought.

"Hey, I have an idea," Dad said suddenly. "Want to watch a movie tonight? Your pick. We could make popcorn and ice cream sundaes!"

Fiona had to smile to herself. She knew full well that Dad wasn't a big fan of movies; he'd rather spend a Saturday night poring over a new volume of poetry. But she appreciated the effort all the same.

"I'm actually pretty tired," she said. "But another time, definitely."

"Sure," Dad said. "Whenever you want."

"I think I'll go upstairs after we finish the dishes," Fiona said. "I kind of want to read for a little while before bed."

"That's a great idea," Dad replied. "I'll do the dishes tonight. You've had a big day—and tomorrow will be even bigger."

Fiona glanced up in alarm. "You know?" she exclaimed.

Dad nodded. "Your teacher Ms. Therian called me this afternoon," he said. "She explained that you might not be able to tell me about the mission, but she said, as your father, I deserved to know that you're going to the *selkies'* isles."

"Are you going to let me go?" Fiona asked, clenching her fists so hard that her fingernails dug into her palms.

Dad tilted his head and stared at her. "Could I stop you if I tried?"

"Probably not," admitted Fiona.

"That's what I thought," he replied.

Fiona stared at the table, unsure of what to say.

"I know there may be things that you can't tell me," Dad continued. "But you can tell your mom, and whenever you need me, Fiona, I'll be here for you."

Then he crossed the room and kissed her forehead. "Don't stay up too late reading," he warned. "I want you to be well rested for . . . whatever tomorrow might bring."

"Don't worry, Dad. I'll go to bed soon," Fiona promised. "Good night."

Moments later Fiona climbed into bed and opened *The Compendium*. The yellowed pages, with their ornate script and detailed illuminations, were familiar in ways that felt almost comforting to Fiona. At this point, she'd read *The Compendium* from cover to cover more times than she could count. And yet, each time she opened it, Fiona felt like she always stumbled upon a new fact or piece of Changer lore that she hadn't known before.

"*Selkies* . . . ," Fiona whispered to herself as her bright green eyes scanned the text. She turned the page, and the words shivered, the letters spiraled across the parchment, rearranging themselves to form all new words. . . .

Selkie Songs

The type of Waterborne Changer known as the selkie, or seal-being, is Unique in its strange ability to use the power of Song in its magic. Such Songs are carefully guarded by selkie-kind, and neither pleading nor threatening can compel a selkie to disclose the Secrets of their Songs. It is a Strange Truth that these Songs are, for all their Secrecy, quite Common. Many Changers and

even Humans have heard their ancient Melodies,
frequently mistaking them for the Songs of Whales
or other Sea Beasts.

A puzzled frown crossed Fiona's face. *So selkie songs*
sound like whale songs, she thought.

Fiona turned the page. To her delight, the words
trembled and rearranged themselves again, revealing
another entry about *selkies* that she'd never seen before.

Dachaigh

One Song of the selkie-kind is called "Dachaigh."
It is a Call for Homecoming known to all selkies.
The moment a selkie enters the Sea, she will Hear
its delicate notes, even through the Roughest
Waters. "Dachaigh" will lead a selkie to her Queen
from any Oceanic point in the world. All she must
do is Follow the notes of the Song. "Dachaigh" also
means that selkies can always find their Queen,
who is entrusted with the most Powerful of all
selkie Songs, one with the ability to Bind, Break,
and Destroy.

Fiona flipped the page eagerly, but the entry ended abruptly, with no further information about *selkies* or their songs. *Oh, come on!* she thought in frustration. What did *The Compendium* mean by "the most Powerful of all *selkie* Songs?" Was that the weapon Ms. Therian had told her about, the song that Fiona needed to convince her mother to use in the battle against Auden Ironbound?

She *had* to learn more. She *had* to know.

But even though Fiona spent hours poring over each page in *The Compendium*, the words were still and unmoving. The book itself felt different in her lap; lighter, less intense. It was like *The Compendium* had closed itself, even though its covers were wide open.

The bedside lamp was still blazing when Fiona finally fell into an exhausted, uneasy sleep. It felt like just minutes later that Dad was gently shaking her shoulder, saying "Fiona? Wake up, Fee," in a low voice near her ear.

"What time is it?" Fiona asked, rubbing her bleary eyes. She reached for *The Compendium* and gently closed its worn leather cover.

"It's time," Dad replied—and that was all he needed

to say for Fiona to remember her mission, set to begin at dawn. She hadn't closed the curtains last night, and now she could see that the night sky had begun to lighten to an inky shade of blue.

"Am I late?" Fiona asked anxiously as she scrambled out of bed.

"No," Dad replied. "Your teacher just arrived. She's waiting downstairs."

"Ms. Therian's *here*?" Fiona said.

Dad nodded. "Go ahead and get dressed," he said.

Then Dad left the room, but even after he was gone, Fiona felt like she could still hear his words reverberating in the air.

It's time.

The cobwebs cleared from her sleep-deprived brain. Fiona dressed in a rush, her heart pounding furiously. It was overwhelming: Fiona's first solo mission—her first trip alone into *selkie* territory—her first chance to speak with her mother in almost ten years.

She tucked The Compendium under her arm and then paused to take a deep, steadying breath. This was it.

And Fiona was ready.

When Fiona entered the living room, Ms. Therian and Dad were standing together in a strained silence; Fiona imagined that they didn't have much to say to each other. They both looked relieved to see her.

"I have *The Compendium*," Fiona said to Ms. Therian. "Thank you for letting me borrow it last night."

"Of course," Ms. Therian said. "I trust that it told you everything you need to know."

"I hope so," Fiona replied, wondering what other secrets about *selkies* the book might hold—and when it would reveal them to her.

"We mustn't tarry," Ms. Therian said crisply. "The sun will be up soon."

"Okay," Dad said. "Let's go."

Then, to Fiona's surprise, Dad turned to her with his hand extended. Suddenly she remembered all the times she had held his hand when she was small—crossing a busy street, splashing through the waves, watching a scary movie. That seemed so long ago, but the moment Fiona took her father's hand, she felt calmer.

I *can do this*, she thought as the three of them began the short walk to the ocean. Her training, her missions, her hours in the saltwater pool at school: it had all been leading up to this moment.

"Listen," Dad said as they arrived at the shoreline. There was an unusual urgency in his voice. "I want you to stay safe. Don't talk to any other Changers—not even if they offer you help. Swim straight for your mother and don't stop until you reach her, do you understand?"

"Yes," she replied. "I do."

"Fiona, what I'm about to tell you is essential," Ms. Therian began. "The *selkies* must *not* know that you've been sent by Changers. If they think that the First Four are using you as some kind of pawn or spy . . ."

Fiona frowned. "What do you—"

"If anyone asks, tell them that you've come to find your mother," Ms. Therian interrupted her.

"So . . . you want me to lie?" asked Fiona.

"No, not lie, exactly—" Dad began.

Ms. Therian spoke over him. "Yes. That's exactly what I'm telling you to do. Your safety, Fiona—and I know your father agrees with me—is of the utmost importance. I cannot stress that enough. Do whatever it takes to protect yourself. *Whatever it takes.*"

Fiona nodded.

"Keep your wits about you," Ms. Therian continued. "For *selkies*, time loses all meaning in the ocean. If you lose focus, it might feel like mere minutes have slipped away, only for you to return and discover that a decade has passed. And your father is right: no matter what, do *not* speak to any other Changers you might encounter. With Auden Ironbound approaching, there's no telling who might be lurking in these waters or which Changers might be sympathetic to his cause."

"I understand," Fiona said. Then she reached forward and embraced Ms. Therian in a hug. Ms. Therian rocked back on her heels, momentarily taken aback— but within a second she was returning Fiona's hug just as tightly.

Fiona turned to her father next. He wrapped his arms around her before she could reach for him. "See you tonight, Fee," he whispered. "I'll be right here, waiting for you."

"See you tonight," Fiona replied, glad that he couldn't see the tears in her eyes.

The pink glow of the rising sun lit up the sky as

Fiona pulled away from her father. She approached the ocean without a single backward glance. When the cold water lapped at her ankles, Fiona wrapped the *selkie* cloak across her shoulders and spun around in the surf.

It was that easy.

For a moment she completely forgot about her father and Ms. Therian standing on the shore, watching her disappear beneath the choppy waves. How could Fiona spare a thought for them when her heart was close to bursting? The joy she felt taking her *selkie* form, diving and darting through the open ocean, was impossible to describe.

It was everything.

Fiona could've surfaced, could've breathed in the salty sea air, but what would be the point? She could hold her breath underwater longer and longer. Besides, she didn't need air the same way now, not the way she needed the water.

Not the way she needed her mother.

The song was calling her.

"*Dachaigh.*"

Louder, clearer, and sweeter than ever. Somehow,

someway, Fiona just *knew* that was her mother's voice.

It felt like she was singing for Fiona and Fiona alone.

The very thought filled Fiona with such joy that she breached the waves in a graceful leap. It was better than running or jumping or skipping; it was even better, Fiona guessed, than flying. Darren could keep the wide blue skies; Fiona had the ocean, and that was the only thing she would ever want in this world.

I'm coming, Mom, Fiona thought, wishing she could sing those words in the language of the *selkies*, hoping that her thoughts could somehow reach her mother across the many miles of ocean between them. Then she swam freely, her heart filled with happiness. There was a soothing sameness to the waves. Before long, Fiona could anticipate each one before it reached her, and she relaxed into them, letting them carry her farther and farther from shore, until at last all she could see was the vast blueness around her: sea and sky, sky and sea.

Fiona swam. On and on and on.

Then, there it was: a solid smudge against the horizon that somehow seemed to grow larger as the compelling notes of "Dachaigh" grew louder.

Land.

By ancient instinct, Fiona knew where she was. These were the Isles of Saorsie, the *selkies'* homeland on this side of the world. And it felt like home already, even though she'd never set foot on those islands.

The waters grew shallower as Fiona approached. Soon, she could brush against the sandy bottom and still keep her head above water. Fiona could see steel-gray rocks jutting out from the water; they seemed to lead toward a cluster of small islands. The rocks were covered with seals, dozens of seals, all basking in the golden sunlight, all watching Fiona's approach.

Somehow, she sensed that they'd known she was coming all along.

When Fiona finally reached the shore and shook off her cloak, she was stunned to see that the sun was already past its peak. I *must've been swimming for eight hours or more*, she thought, *but it only felt like minutes.*

Along the sandbars and rocky outcrops near the shore, the *selkies* began to change into their human forms: men with shell necklaces, and women with elaborately braided hair, all wearing cloaks of different colors. Never once did their eyes leave Fiona as she began walking up the beach. *Is Mom among them?* she wondered. *What if I don't recognize her?*

Fiona grew more nervous with every step; she didn't even notice when some of the *selkies* began to bow to her. A beautiful woman stepped out from a rocky cave at the island's heart. She wore a tiara of coral and pearls; a luxurious copper cloak hung from her shoulders. The woman's green eyes glowed with warmth; her brilliant red hair blazed. But nothing was brighter than the love that radiated from her face.

Fiona didn't need to worry.

She recognized her mother at once.

Chapter 6
THE SELKIE QUEEN

Fiona had been dreaming of this moment since she'd first learned that her mother was alive, but now that she was living it, she wasn't sure what to do. Her feet were rooted to the sand as she stared at her mother—so beautiful, so *alive*—in disbelief. Should she run to her? Hug her? Curtsy? Drop to the sand in a deep bow?

Her mother crossed the sand with smooth, elegant strides and took Fiona in her arms as if it were the most natural thing in the world. "My girl, you've come home to me," the queen said.

The memories came rushing back to Fiona: her mother's soft skin, the feel of her strong arms, the whiff of gardenia that perfumed her hair. She hadn't forgotten her mother at all; the memories had been safely tucked away in her heart.

That's when the tears came. But Mom didn't seem to mind; she rocked Fiona and sang to her just the way she had when Fiona was a little baby. And even now, it made Fiona feel better—just like it used to.

"Mom," Fiona said, trying the word out. It felt good to say it aloud after so long. "Mom. I never thought we'd be together again."

"Oh, Fiona," her mother said. "I've always been near, watching over you. How proud I've been, all these years, seeing you grow into such a fine person. How good it feels to tell you that at last."

Mom brushed the tears from Fiona's face, beaming at her. "Come," she said, taking Fiona by the hand. "We have a lot of catching up to do."

Fiona expected her mother to take her to the cave, but instead, Queen Leana brought her down the beach, away from the *selkies'* curious eyes. Small, twisted pines that had been sculpted by hard winds and salty ocean spray sheltered this side of the island. It was cooler, calmer, and quieter—the perfect place for a long heart-to-heart talk.

But that wasn't what Mom had in mind either.

"I know you had a long journey to get here," she began. "But would you like to go for a swim?"

"With you?" Fiona exclaimed. "Yes! Of course!"

"You're not too tired?" asked Mom.

"Not at all," Fiona assured her.

"Follow me, then." She clutched her cloak more tightly around her shoulders and transformed in one seamless motion, and there she was: the copper-colored seal with the bright, intelligent eyes that Fiona had seen so many times before.

Your turn, Mom thought to Fiona.

Fiona had never felt prouder to wrap her precious cloak across her shoulders than under her mother's approving gaze. After she took her seal form, Fiona realized that she was a full head shorter than her mother. *I guess even my selkie form still has some growing to do*, she thought.

Fiona followed her mother into the azure waters. The seas were calm, making it even easier for Fiona to bob and spin through the sun-dappled water. She and her mother raced together, over and under the waves, and it felt, for a moment, like they'd never been apart. *Maybe that's the magic of the water,* Fiona thought as she heard her mother humming a beautiful melody. *Or maybe that's the magic of the* selkies, *that time loses all meaning here and all the pain of the past washes away with it.*

After a while Fiona realized that Mom was guiding her back to shore. She still wasn't tired—she wondered briefly if it was even possible for *selkies* to get tired from swimming—but she had a feeling that she and her mother were going to talk.

Back on the soft white sands, Mom sat down and squeezed the water from Fiona's long hair, then used her fingers to comb out the tangles. Fiona closed her eyes and basked in the warmth of the sun as her mother began to braid her hair in the style Fiona had seen on the *selkies* on the beach.

"I can imagine what you must be thinking," Mom began. "All these years, gone . . . Why? Why didn't I come for you? Why didn't I find a way to contact you when I was so close the whole time?"

Fiona nodded.

"I certainly can't blame you. I would be wondering the same things. I'll do my best to explain.

"We are descended from a royal bloodline," Mom continued. "But for a thousand years that was nothing more than a quaint tidbit of *selkie* lore—ancient history, you might say. Under the leadership of the First Four, the *selkies* were just another part of the Changer nation. We had no need for a queen of our own anymore. It became a ceremonial title only, and over time, even that faded into nothingness. Which was all right with me."

"You didn't want to be queen?" asked Fiona.

Mom laughed, a beautiful, clear sound like the ringing of a bell. "No, never!" she exclaimed. "It was wonderfully freeing. I was the great-great-great-granddaughter of the last queen, but my life was my own. I could go where I wanted, do what I wanted, be whoever I wanted to be. And I was never more grateful for that than when I fell in love with your father. There was nothing to stand in our way . . . certainly not my lineage.

"But discontent was brewing among the *selkies*," Mom explained. "We've always been proud, you know.

It's not one of our better qualities. And some among us began to feel that our relationship with other Changers was . . . exploitative, I suppose, would be the best word."

Fiona frowned. "Why did the *selkies* think that?"

"The *selkies* had fought in the Changers' wars and used their magic to establish the Changer nation," Mom told her. "But there was no *selkie* included in the First Four's leadership council. I don't believe it was intentional, but that slight didn't sit well with our kind. They felt they'd sacrificed a great deal and received little in return. They were adamant that we didn't need the Changers' protection—or even their friendship."

Fiona felt as though there had to be something she was missing here; couldn't all this have been settled with a simple meeting? Fiona prepared to speak, but Mom held up a finger.

"I know you're a student of Dorina Therian; I've always had great respect for the First Four," she said. "But you must try to understand the concerns of your kind. *Selkies* fought valiantly, undertook the most dangerous missions, created magical objects without question, and freely shared the power of our songs. Yet we were excluded from leadership, never allowed to know all the details. Why were we fighting? *Who* were we fighting? What were our enchanted objects being used for?"

Fiona stared at the horizon, deep in thought. *I can see their point,* she admitted to herself.

"You were three years old when a messenger arrived at our cottage," Mom continued in a quiet voice. "Calls for violence were escalating, and it was rumored that the *selkies* were ready to fight for their freedom. We were on the brink of war. The messenger begged me to return to the homeland with her. 'We need our queen,' she said. 'We need royal blood to show us the way. To lead us.' All I had to do, Fiona, was return. They had already pledged their loyalty to me."

"So that's why you left," Fiona said.

"Not exactly," her mother replied. "I have always been against violence. If I could help prevent a war, I knew in my heart it was my duty to do so—not just for my kind, but for all the world . . . and *especially* for you and your father. A war among Changers would be a terrible thing for non-magical beings. So I returned to the Isles of Saorsie as a voice for peace.

"The *selkies* welcomed me as their queen from the start," Mom said. "They allowed me to negotiate with the First Four to gain our freedom without a single battle. When I signed the treaty that secured our independence, it was one of the proudest moments of my life. As the ink dried I dreamed of returning home—to my husband, to my baby, to the life I'd made for myself."

"I don't understand," Fiona said, a look of puzzlement on her face. "What went wrong?"

"The *selkies* were too unstable to be left to their own devices," Mom told her. "There were factions who simply couldn't agree on anything—except my role as their rightful queen. They needed a leader, a mediator. My advisers told me in no uncertain terms that our new nation would crumble if I left for the mainland. In my heart I knew they were right. And I also knew that I couldn't lead two lives: one at sea, one on land; one as a *selkie*, one as a human."

Fiona already knew what was coming, but she dreaded hearing about what happened next.

"I went home for just one day," Mom said, her voice halting. "I hid your cloak to keep it safe for when you would come of age. I forced your father to swear to tell you I'd died; I didn't want you to try searching for me until the time was right. And there were things set in motion that, even now, I can't yet tell you about. Suffice it to say, this was the only way I could fulfill my duty— and save my kind. I promised that I'd return when you came into your powers. When you were old enough to understand what I'd done and why. You must believe me that I always planned to come back to you, Fiona. Who else would teach you the *selkie* ways, our songs and stories?"

"Sure," Fiona said. "I believe you." But there was a hard edge to her voice, and she couldn't meet her mother's eyes.

"Go ahead, Fiona," Mom said gently, letting go of the intricate braids she'd made in Fiona's wet hair. "You can say it."

Fiona struggled to find the right words. "It's just— It— It didn't have to be this way!" she cried. "I don't just need you *now*, Mom. I needed you always. Every day you were gone, I needed you!"

A long silence followed.

When Fiona finally mustered the courage to turn around to look at her mother, she was stunned to see tears streaming down Mom's face.

"Forgive me," Mom said. "I know I'm asking a lot of you, Fiona; more than I have a right to ask. But if there's any way you can find it in your heart to forgive me. . . . For years this decision has destroyed me inside. Not a day's gone by that I haven't regretted it, wrestled with my choices, second-guessed *everything*, searched in vain for a solution, a compromise. I am confident that if there was *any* other way, I would've found it long ago. No one could've tried harder than me.

"Our family has paid dearly for my lineage," Mom continued. "My duties to my kind tore me away from my duties to you. But don't you see? Those dark days are behind us now. There's nothing that can keep us apart. I'm determined to teach you everything about being a *selkie*. We have so much lost time to make up for—and now we have all the time in the world."

There was a part of Fiona that was still trying to work out how she felt about her mom; something inside her wanted to shout, *You should have found a way to stay with us!* But seeing her mom in tears seemed to drown out all the anger. Just twenty-four hours ago, Fiona didn't even know her mother was alive. Now her mom was here, wanting so desperately to be not just a mother, but also a teacher, a guide for all the abilities Fiona needed to learn. Fiona knew that it was enough, at least for now.

"I forgive you, Mom," Fiona whispered as she reached for her mother. "I—I probably would've made the same choice. And we're together now. That's really all that matters."

But even as her mother gathered her in a warm embrace, a nagging feeling tugged at Fiona's heart. Even on the Isles of Saorsie, a world that felt about a million miles from Willow Cove, Fiona couldn't forget about Auden Ironbound . . . and the real reason for her mission.

Chapter 7
THE PRELUDE

The doorbell rang before dawn on Sunday.

Mack had only been asleep for a few hours, but he jolted upright and jumped out of bed, stumbling over his own feet as he reached for the light. "Ow!" Mack yelped, grabbing his stubbed toe. He could hear Jiichan's soft footsteps moving through the hallway. By the time Mack got to the front door, Jiichan had already escorted in a pair of anxious-looking Changers.

"We're so sorry about the hour," a man said. "We couldn't wait any longer."

A woman clutched a bundle to her chest; Mack realized it was a sleeping baby.

"You're safe now," Jiichan said soothingly. "Please, come into my study. Make yourselves comfortable. Makoto, if you would put the kettle on? I think a nice cup of tea first, and then we will discuss your options." Then, with a reassuring smile, he led the couple down the hall.

Before the kettle was boiling, Jiichan came into the kitchen. His brown eyes were troubled. "It begins, Makoto," he said in a grave voice.

"The attack?" Mack asked, suddenly alert.

"The prelude," Jiichan corrected him. "Changers from all over will start arriving. Some will be ready to fight Auden Ironbound, and some will be seeking our protection. The day will be long, and I will need your help."

"Anything. Of course," Mack said eagerly. "I can draft battle strategies and draw maps for escape routes and—"

"Make tea," interrupted Jiichan.

Mack's face fell. "'Make tea'?" he repeated with confusion.

"Our visitors will be scared, stressed, exhausted. A cup of comforting tea is precisely what they will need to fortify them for the difficulties that lie ahead. I want you to keep the kettle boiling at all times. Open the door, offer them tea, and escort them to the living room to wait for me. I will meet with each arrival separately."

Mack opened his mouth to ask a question, but Jiichan cut in first.

"The door is enchanted against enemies," Jiichan said. "You needn't worry about warlocks in disguise."

"All right. If that's what you want me to do, sure," Mack said, hoping he was able to hide his disappointment. In his heart, he wanted a more exciting, important job than door opening and tea making . . . but he knew that his wants weren't the priority right now.

Ding-dong.

Jiichan raised his eyebrows at Mack and then nodded toward the front entryway. Mack understood.

It really had begun.

As Jiichan disappeared into his study, Mack hurried to the door and opened it wide. A middle-aged man stood on the step, the streetlights glinting off his bald head. Mack was sure he'd never met him before, but the man seemed to recognize him right away.

"What an honor," he said as he vigorously shook Mack's hand. "I heard all about your triumph on the beach, Makoto. Amazing! Though I guess no one should be surprised, considering who your grandfather is."

"Uh, thanks," Mack said, a little surprised. It wasn't the first time he'd been recognized, and Mack knew that he'd never get used to it.

Before the man had even stepped inside, Mack saw a woman hurrying up to the walkway. "Please, come in," he said, remembering Jiichan's words. "You're welcome here."

"Good," the woman said. "Because I'm ready to fight with you and the First Four and any other Changer brave enough to defy Auden."

Mack ping-ponged between the kitchen, the front door, and the living room, pouring endless cups of tea for more Changers than he'd ever met before. Again and again, Mack was asked if he would be battling Auden Ironbound, and each time it got harder to answer. Mack didn't even want to think about it, but he was powerless to push the thought from his mind: *What if Jiichan is right? What if Auden Ironbound has new defenses against me—or new weapons to use?*

What if I let everyone down?

It was too terrible to think about—especially when so many Changers seemed to be counting on him.

By midmorning, Mack was ready for a break, but the doorbell just kept ringing. He was surprised when he opened it the next time to find Gabriella and Darren standing on the doorstep.

"Hey!" Mack exclaimed as a grin spread across his face. "What are you guys doing here?"

"We're going downtown for a while," Darren explained. "Want to come?"

"With everything going on, Tía Rosa decided to stay for the weekend," Gabriella added, pointing at a silver car idling in the driveway. The driver honked and waved through the window.

"Seriously?" Mack cried. "Your aunt's coming too?" It was no secret that Mack, a huge fan of superhero comics, had been a little starstruck from the moment he realized that Gabriella's aunt had been a superhero called the Emerald Wildcat.

"She had some errands to run and said we could tag along," said Gabriella.

"Hang on," Mack said. "I'll be right back."

The next time Jiichan emerged from his study, Mack asked for permission to go out for a while.

"Yes, you have earned a break," Jiichan told him. "Yara is on her way now to help. Please, be careful. Stay with your friends at all times. There is safety in numbers . . . especially now."

"I will," Mack promised. "Thanks, Jiichan. I'll be home soon."

Minutes later, Ms. Rivera parked the car on Market Street. "I'm going to get some coffee," she said, stifling a yawn. "Meet you back at the car in thirty minutes?"

"You got it," Gabriella replied. She gave her aunt a quick wave and then turned to Mack and Darren. "Want to see if the bookstore has any new comics?"

"Definitely," Mack agreed. "They usually get shipments on Fridays. Maybe we'll even run into Joel there!" Joel was Mack's best friend; he didn't have any magical abilities, but none of that mattered to Mack. He started to follow Gabriella but then realized that Darren was lagging behind. "Hey," Mack called. "You coming?"

"Yeah. Sorry," he said. "I thought I saw . . . Never mind. It was nothing."

"Jiichan told me we have to stick together," Mack said. Darren just nodded in response.

In the quiet of the bookstore, surrounded by ordinary people browsing for books, it was almost possible to forget about the looming battle. Almost, but not quite. Every so often Mack would feel a jolt when he remembered what was happening at home. The trip to town wasn't quite the distraction he had hoped for.

He closed the comic book he picked up and tucked it under his arm. "I just read the same page three times, and I still can't tell you what happened," he whispered.

"Yeah," Gabriella said. "I'm having trouble concentrating too."

"Let's get something to eat," Darren suggested. "Then we can talk."

While Mack paid for his comic, Darren and Gabriella bought some cookies from the bookstore's cafe. Then they found a table where they could talk privately.

"I can't stop thinking about Fiona," Gabriella began.

"Where do you think she is right now? Do you think she's made it to the Isles of Saorsie yet?"

Darren checked the time on his phone. "Maybe," he said. "But it seemed like even Ms. Therian didn't know exactly how far away it was." Then he turned to Mack. "Did your grandfather say anything to you?"

"Honestly, we've barely even had a chance to talk today," Mack told his friends. "The doorbell started ringing while it was still dark. It's been nonstop, one Changer after another."

"So they're taking Auden Ironbound seriously?" asked Gabriella.

"Very seriously," Mack said. "Some of them are scared; some of them are angry. And I mean *really* angry. They came here ready to fight."

"Good," Darren said. "I think we're gonna need all the help we can get."

"I don't know about that," Gabriella said. "Tía Rosa is, like, supremely unconcerned."

"Well, yeah," Mack joked. "Because she's a *superhero*."

Gabriella smiled, but she shook her head. "I guess it's possible that she's putting on an act so I don't freak out," she said. "But last night she told me all about the Harbors."

Mack sat up a little straighter. "'The Harbors'?" he repeated. "You mean Middletown Marina?"

Gabriella shook her head again. "No. The Harbors are top secret Changer bases in Willow Cove and around the country that can protect all of us," she explained. "They're pretty much impenetrable. So if the worst happens, there's a fallback plan, at least."

"I don't get it," said Darren. "How come the First Four didn't open up the Harbors the last time Auden Ironbound attacked?"

"Probably because it was a sneak attack," Mack said wisely. "Remember how Auden Ironbound showed up early, before anybody was expecting him? Plus, the First Four didn't even know the truth about the Horn of Power. They thought they'd still be immune."

Gabriella crossed her arms and hugged herself. "This is what scares me," she said. "What we know is bad enough. But it's what we *don't* know that's really dangerous."

"Yeah," Mack said, nodding slowly. "All the Changers who came over this morning . . . They all think that I can beat Auden Ironbound again, just because I did it before."

Darren let out a low whistle. "Man," he said. "That's a lot of pressure."

"The truth is, none of us *really* knows what Auden Ironbound can do," Mack continued. "I mean, the First Four are concerned. That's enough for me."

A worried expression flickered across Gabriella's face. "Maybe Tía Rosa isn't being cautious enough," she said. "We should . . . find her."

"You okay?" asked Darren.

"I'm not sure," Gabriella admitted. "I suddenly have a very weird feeling about everything."

"Let's go," Mack said, standing so abruptly that his chair screeched as it slid across the floor.

Looking back, he would always wonder when, exactly, it had happened. Was it while they were walking to the door, or was it the moment they stepped outside? Everything seemed the same at first, but the light— there was something wrong with it—had a greenish tinge, and the air was unusually still.

Not just the air, though. The clouds were frozen in

the sky; the leaves were motionless on the trees. And the people . . .

The people were the worst part of it all.

The sidewalks were still crowded with them; people were seated in unmoving cars, but there was something so fundamentally odd, so *wrong*, that Mack had an over-whelming urge to run away as far and as fast as he could, and never look back. They were completely stiff and unmoving, like horrible frozen mannequins. When Mack forced himself to look closer, he realized that they were breathing slowly, steadily, and in perfect, chilling unison.

But that seemed to be all they could do.

"It's a curse," Darren whispered. "They're cursed. We've got to get out of here!"

"Not without Tía Rosa!" Gabriella snapped anxiously, scanning the crowd.

"We should—" Mack began.

Then he saw it out of the corner of his eye: a flash of movement. A woman, dressed all in black, was moving supernaturally fast toward them, her hand held high as a glimmering orb began to form in her palm.

"Look out!" Mack screamed.

Darren was already on it, a sizzling bolt of electricity jumping from finger to finger as he channeled all his energy into making the strongest lightning bolt of his life. It glowed white-hot—then burst into a million smaller bolts, each one sizzling as they linked together to form a powerful force field, a web of pure, unbridled electrical power—

Suddenly, Darren doubled over, as if he'd been punched in the stomach. He fell to his knees, breathless, and Mack saw a magic-user behind Darren, holding him hostage.

Gabriella transformed so quickly that she was just a blur of black fur. She lunged forward, leaping over the unmoving people as she charged at Darren's attacker.

Mack was just one step behind her, on the verge of transforming himself when there was a sudden sharp pain in his elbows, as if they were being pinned behind his back.

He twisted his neck, trying to see who had grabbed him.

A choking cloud of smoke surrounded him . . .

And everything went black.

Chapter 8
CURSED

The moment Gabriella attacked, Darren's captor released him. In an instant Darren transformed. With a little height, he would be able to cast an even wider force field to protect him and his friends from the attack. He flapped his massive wings once and propelled himself up onto the bookstore's awning. Darren's piercing eyes glinted as he surveyed the scene below. *One—two—three.* He counted the figures as they crept among the statue-people.

The cloud of smoke sprang up so suddenly that Darren didn't know exactly where it came from or how it happened. All he knew was that one moment Mack was standing there, ready to fight, and the next moment he was on the ground.

Mack! Darren's cry ripped through his thoughts.

But there was no answer.

Then Darren saw something so horrifying that a piercing bird-shriek escaped him, shattering the bookstore's window. Before, he thought he'd seen . . . But it was over so fast, he couldn't be sure. . . .

Now, though, there was no doubt: Jasper, Auden Ironbound's most devoted follower, crept in beside the warlocks. His tall, gaunt form cast a long, terrible shadow that seemed to grow with every step he took.

What's wrong? Gabriella thought frantically.

Jasper's here, Darren replied, peering through the clearing smoke with his keen eyes. *They did something to Mack—* Gabriella! Look out!

Gabriella spun, her front paw already raised with her dagger-sharp claws revealed. The sight was enough to make the witch creeping up behind her turn and run.

There was a series of popping sounds, followed by more billowing clouds of smoke.

Darren flapped his wings, trying to clear away the

air so he could see what was happening below.

Give me the big picture, Gabriella's voice rang through Darren's head. *Who's coming at me?*

There were five witches and warlocks, not including Jasper, Darren thought. *There's one warlock crouching behind that red car; I think the others are gone. But Jasper . . . I can't see through the smoke. Be careful . . .*

Even from above, Darren could hear Gabriella's menacing growl as she crouched low to the ground. He clicked his talons together, generating a tornado of blazing sparks. If Gabriella needed backup, Darren would be ready to blast her attacker with a lightning bolt.

Not that she'll need it, he thought.

A motion down the street caught his eye. Someone— something—was moving fast. A black blur . . .

Darren was ready to attack when he realized that the dark blur wasn't a warlock at all.

It was Gabriella's aunt, charging forward in her *nahual* form.

Darren sucked in his breath sharply. He'd never seen *two nahuals* together before. Gabriella and her aunt were creatures of unspeakable power.

The one remaining warlock certainly thought so. There was another puff of smoke, and then—just like that—he was gone.

What happened? Ms. Rivera's words ricocheted through Darren's mind as he threw a lightning bolt.

It's Jasper. He's here, Gabriella replied.

As if he'd heard his name, Jasper seemed to appear from the last traces of smoke. His thin, colorless lips parted in an oily smile. "Rosa! How good to see you," he sneered. "I'm not much of a cat person, but I'll make an exception for someone so *super*."

The roar that escaped from Ms. Rivera's throat was loud enough to rip the world apart. Jasper's arrogant smirk faltered for a moment. Was that fear in his eyes?

Darren saw Jasper's wormy lips begin to move; he was mumbling something under his breath. . . .

Tía Rosa, Gabriella thought. *What's happening?*

Darren watched in horror as Gabriella's fur began to fade to a dull gray. The same thing happened to her aunt.

A curse! Darren thought frantically.

His talons scratched against one another as he started forming another lightning bolt, putting all his anger into the work. Darren didn't have time to second-guess it. He aimed squarely at Jasper and threw it. With nimble speed Jasper stepped aside just in time to avoid a direct hit, but the bolt sliced through the edge of his sleeve, leaving a smoking tear in its wake.

In that moment Jasper was distracted just long enough for Ms. Rivera to lunge. Her claws flashed in the sunlight, there was a horrible rip—not cloth this time, something thicker and more substantial . . .

A splatter of blood arced through the air.

More smoke billowed around them.

Then an unexpected calm settled over the street.

Darren flew down to the ground, transforming in midflight. By the time he landed, Gabriella and Ms. Rivera were in their human forms again too.

Gabriella's aunt scrambled to pick up Mack, who was lying still on the sidewalk. She lifted him into her arms as though he was weightless, and just in time: The street unfroze, and all the people began to move, like nothing unusual had ever happened.

"Is he—" Darren could barely say the words.

"No," Ms. Rivera said. "He's alive. But I've never seen

a curse like this. We need to get him back to Akira, now."

Ms. Rivera rushed back to the car and buckled Mack, upright, into the backseat. Darren jumped in beside him while Gabriella and her aunt settled in up front.

"They snuck up on us," Darren whispered as he looked over at Mack.

"It was so fast," Gabriella said, her hand over her heart as she tried to take a steadying breath. "So fast."

Ms. Rivera started the car, and Darren tried not to watch the speedometer as the needle crept up past forty, fifty, even sixty miles an hour. It wasn't Ms. Rivera's speeding that bothered him.

It was that she thought driving so fast was necessary.

Darren's stomach lurched when they arrived at Mack's house and parked, knowing that they were about to break the terrible news to Mr. Kimura. Darren glanced at Gabriella out of the corner of his eye. *Was it like this for everybody else when the warlocks took me?* he wondered.

Ms. Rivera, getting out of the car and carrying Mack, pushed past Darren and kicked on the door loudly.

Mr. Kimura opened it, the look of calm melting off his face. His shoulders sagged as he rushed them indoors.

They crowded into the front hallway, and Yara poked her head out of the kitchen. "Thank goodness you're back," she began. "If I never see another pot of tea . . ."

Her voice trailed off unexpectedly as she noticed Mack. "What happened?" she asked.

"Not here," Mr. Kimura said quietly.

As they hurried down the hall, Darren caught a glimpse of the living room, which was crowded with Changers he'd never seen before. *Wow. Mack wasn't kidding,* he thought, and felt another twinge of guilt. *If we hadn't come over. If Mack had stayed home to help his grandfather. . . .*

When the rice-paper doors to Mack's room were closed behind them, Ms. Rivera began to speak. "Warlocks. Five of them at least, and Jasper, too. They must have been following us, though they were good enough that even I couldn't sense their presence. They cursed all of Market Street—an immobility curse, I think, or some sort of time freeze—and struck the younglings. Cowards, all of them, but that's no surprise."

As Ms. Rivera laid Mack on his bed, Darren looked up, expecting to see Mr. Kimura's eyes flashing with fury. What he actually saw there, though—a mixture of despair and grief—was about a thousand times worse.

"It's clear to me why they targeted Mack," she continued. "They're afraid of his abilities, of course. They know this will strike a blow to us."

Mr. Kimura and Yara didn't look comforted by Ms. Rivera's theory. "That's only part of it," Yara confessed. "There are other reasons why Auden Ironbound would want to take down Mack. Frankly, I'd be surprised if he was the only target."

Darren's head shot back. "You think they were trying to get us, too?" he asked, gesturing at Gabriella and himself.

"Fiona had a theory," Gabriella began. "She thought— Well, she thought we were stronger when we were together. Is that even possible, though?"

Mr. Kimura nodded slowly. "Fiona was right, but there is more to it. Far more," he explained. "Yara, if you would take Rosa, Gabriella, and Darren into my study. I need quiet to determine what kind of curse this is."

Darren snuck one last look at Mack before turning to follow Yara. When she closed the screen behind them, she brought them in close.

"Mack will be all right," Yara said, trying to cheer

them. "Akira has yet to find a curse he can't undo."

Then her mouth turned upward into a slight grin. "Sefu and Dorina will be quite the picture when they hear we've told you this. We were waiting until you were a bit further along in your training, but time is short, and our hope is growing dimmer. . . ." Her voice trailed off. "A few hundred years ago a prophecy was delivered to us. It foretold the next generation of leadership for Changer-kind."

Darren and Gabriella exchanged a puzzled glance. "What did it say?" asked Darren.

"The exact words I cannot recall, but it led us to you. You see, it is no coincidence that the four of you are here, in Willow Cove, coming of age together. It was foretold long before any of you were born. That's why Dorina is teaching you. It's why all of the First Four are so closely involved in your training. Our time has begun to dwindle, but yours is dawning."

"So you think . . . ," Darren wondered aloud. "Us working together . . . Is that why we were able to beat Auden before?"

"Certainly. It's part of why he has had such a keen interest in you," Yara responded. "He desires to eliminate you, one by one, before the battle even begins."

"But why?" Gabriella burst out. "We're not even fully trained yet."

A crinkled half smile filled Yara's face. "We have been able to hold off threats like him all these years," she explained. "But you . . . Your rise will usher in a new era of peace. We have never known peace, not true peace, since the Horn of Power was first blown some thousand years ago. Auden is not wrong to fear you."

A long silence followed. Darren could tell he wasn't the only one who felt totally overwhelmed by this news. Gabriella's dark eyes were swimming with unasked questions too.

Then he turned to Yara. "I don't mean to be disrespectful, but you can't leave it like this," he told her. "What is this prophecy, exactly? Who foretold it? What if it's all a fake, or some terrible joke—"

"What if it's not even real?" Gabriella broke in.

"Don't we have a right to know?" added Darren.

Yara waited patiently until they finished. Then she said, "Of course you do. And you will know—everything. Provided we survive the next twenty-four hours."

Chapter 9
THE COUNCIL OF ELDERS

When Fiona and her mother returned from the other side of the island, the sun had begun its descent, casting long, mysterious shadows across the sand. Glowing conch shells, no doubt lit with magic, dotted the shore, marking a path that led to the open mouth of the cave. One of the *selkies* hurried up to them, sweeping into a low curtsy as she approached. "Your Majesty," she said.

"You may rise, Una," Mom said.

Una stood and carefully adjusted Mom's tiara and then added heavy ropes of pearls around her neck. With her gleaming *selkie* cloak, Mom looked more regal and elegant than Fiona ever could've imagined.

"Your advisers have arrived," Una said. "The council awaits your presence."

"Very good," Mom replied. "I will be there directly."

"If I may, Your Majesty," Una began. "It might be preferable for Princess Fiona to wait for you outside. I would be honored to attend to her while you are occupied."

Princess? Fiona thought, trying not to laugh.

"Thank you, but that won't be necessary," Mom told her. "This is Fiona's birthright. It is never too early for her to study at the table of diplomacy or to learn the ways of our council."

Una's eyes flickered with worry. "But—"

"She has every right to be there," Mom said firmly.

"Yes, Your Majesty," Una replied. "Of course. I beg your pardon."

With Mom's arm across her shoulders, Fiona walked up the conch-lit path toward the cave. Inside, the cavern blazed with hundreds of burning torches, but even they weren't enough to completely chase away the darkness and the damp. In the center of the cave was a long, low table made out of driftwood that had been lashed together with thick cords of rope. *Sailor's knots,* Fiona thought briefly, then shifted her focus to Mom. She swept through the room with her head held high; her copper hair gleamed like a sunset-lit waterfall. There was a quiet murmur among the *selkies* as Mom passed; then, silence. It was obvious that all the *selkies* had a deep respect for their queen.

Mom took her place at the head of the table, where there was an ornate throne made of driftwood. Even among the high ceremony, Leana didn't forget about her daughter. Mom smiled warmly at her as she gestured to a chair beside her. It was smaller and shorter than the other chairs at the table; Fiona had a feeling it had been added at the last minute, just for her.

Once Mom took her place at the head of the table, all the other *selkies* bowed their heads. Fiona did too—but she kept her eyes open, watching closely.

"Children of the sea, we gather here tonight as a council of *selkies*," Mom said in a somber voice. "May the moon pull us to the correct conclusions; may the wind whisper wisdom in our ears; may the tides turn our hearts to justice in all matters that come before this council—tonight and for all time."

"May it be," the other *selkies* chorused.

"The timepiece," Mom said, holding out her hand.

Una scurried forward, carrying an elaborate hour-glass filled with pure-white sand. Mom took it, turned it upside down, and glanced at the parchment before her.

"Maeve," she called.

A woman at the table with a sable-colored cloak stood up. "I present a petition from our sisters off the Irish coast," she began. "Three islands are in dispute with the Changers, who claim these islands are within the one-league realm from shore, as decided in the Treaty of Fair Passage."

"Are they?" Mom asked in an even voice.

Maeve fidgeted. "Well . . . ," she began, "the islands have been in our possession since before the treaty was signed. Our sisters there feel that they should remain so under the provisions of clause seven, stating that previously settled lands should remain in the hands of their original inhabitants."

A slight frown crossed Mom's face. "Why is this issue coming before the council now?" she asked. "The treaty was signed a decade ago."

"Well, ah, our Irish sisters weren't, um, making use of the islands then," Maeve said. "In fact, they were technically abandoned. But the land-Changers have overreached and begun a settlement. . . . Some sort of base, we believe. The islands are uniquely positioned for that because they are cloaked in mist much of the time, hiding them from human view."

"Would you say that the land dwellers believed these islands to be deserted?" Mom asked.

Now Maeve looked really uncomfortable. "They left a marker," she said awkwardly, "though it may have washed away. . . ."

Mom rolled the pearls from her necklace in her palms, deep in thought. "I have made my decision," she said. "These islands were considered deserted under clause four of the treaty. They have thus passed into the hands of the Changers. Our Irish sisters will not lay further claim to them and will be more careful to exert their presence on any lands they wish to retain under their dominion."

"May it be," the *selkies* chorused as Mom turned the hourglass over.

"Erynn," she said.

A wizened old *selkie* whose silver cloak matched the streaks in her hair rose to her feet. "I bring a petition from our people in Japan," she began. "There is a dispute with the finfolk."

Mom raised an eyebrow. "The mermaids again?" she asked. "Didn't we hear this petition at our last council?"

"Yes, my queen," Erynn replied. "But there have been escalations. The finfolk stole Yuri's cloak and are holding it for ransom."

Mom's eyes were usually a beautiful shade of green, but hearing that news made them darken until they were the color of the sea under a stormy sky. "Have I heard you correctly?" she asked in a dangerously quiet voice. "They *stole* her *cloak*?"

"Yes, Your Majesty."

Mom's verdict was swift and decisive. "I grant permission to attack," she said. "They should use just as much force as necessary to retrieve the cloak and send a message—no more, no less.

"Furthermore, I summon Yuri to next month's council. She should depart as soon as her cloak is returned," Mom continued.

There was a collective gasp of surprise.

"I expect her to stand before us and explain how such a thing happened," Mom said. "If I find out that this was part of a trap to lure the finfolk into an escalation—"

"I'm sure that's not the case," Erynn told Mom.

"Either way, the finfolk will pay," Mom declared. "And in the future, I trust Yuri to be more careful with her cloak. We will not be so fast to start a war for her if it happens again."

Mom turned the hourglass. "Now, we come to the main reason for our council: Auden Ironbound's declaration of war. I trust you all heard his call to action."

The *selkies* around the table nodded.

"Then we must choose our course with great care," Mom continued. "This decision is too large for me to make unilaterally. I want to hear what you think. The floor is open. All who wish to comment will have the opportunity to do so."

"We cannot side with Auden Ironbound," Erynn spoke up immediately. "We cannot even consider it."

A chorus of agreement rose from the other *selkies*. Even Mom was nodding.

"I agree," she said. "He used the Horn of Power against us, which is unforgivable. He who would have us enslaved can never be considered our ally. I hereby decree that any *selkie* who sides with Auden Ironbound shall be banished and his or her cloak destroyed."

Wow, Fiona thought, her eyes wide with horror. That sounded like a punishment worse than death.

"The more complicated item of business is the Changers," a *selkie* called Neely said. "They will go to war, I'm sure of it."

"The First Four enjoy a good fight, so long as they don't have to get their hands dirty," Erynn said with a snide edge in her voice that made Fiona's temper flare. She stayed silent, though, listening intently.

"To join with them would be nothing more than another form of enslavement!" a *selkie*—the only man at the table—said hotly. "*Selkies* are free and independent. We serve no one but ourselves!"

"We owe the Changers no allegiance," another said with a contemptuous sniff. "They're only after our songs."

"Let me ask you this: Would any Changer in the world fight for *us* in a time of war?" still another *selkie* asked.

A collective grumble arose from the *selkies* gathered at the table. Their barely subdued anger took Fiona by surprise. *They* really *don't like the other Changers at all*, she thought, feeling a pang of sadness. Fiona pictured the Changers she knew—Darren and Mack and Gabriella; the First Four. They had only ever treated her with kindness and respect. It was entirely different from the way the *selkies* spoke of them.

"I think we've heard from everyone," Mom finally said. "Unless there are objections, I'm ready to issue a decree. At this time, we will remain neutral. This is not our war, and we will not be engaged to fight in it."

"May it be," replied the other *selkies*—all except one.

"Wait," Fiona said, her voice ringing off the cave walls.

Everyone turned to look at her.

Ms. Therian's warning flashed through her mind. How could she convince the *selkies* to join forces with the other Changers—without making them suspect the truth behind her visit?

"May I speak?" Fiona asked, trying to buy herself a few moments.

"Your Majesty, this is highly improper," Erynn spoke up. "We were happy to indulge her presence during a closed council meeting, but this—"

"Overruled," Mom interrupted, the hint of a smile dancing in her eyes. "I opened the floor to any *selkie* who wished to comment. Naturally, that includes my daughter. Go ahead, Fiona. You may speak."

Fiona slowly rose to her feet, her heart hammering in her chest. Part of her wanted nothing more than to fall back onto her chair in silent safety.

But Fiona was a *selkie*. Not a coward. She would speak—even if it took everything she had.

"I heard Auden Ironbound's message too," Fiona began. "He marches on Willow Cove to start a war against the land-Changers. But what makes us think we can choose the luxury of neutrality? How can we assume he will even give us this choice?"

In the quiet that followed, Fiona found the courage to press on.

"Willow Cove is not far from the Isles of Saorsie," she pointed out. "I am a youngling, and I made the trip in half a day. If the other Changers fall—if Auden Ironbound defeats them—what's to stop him from marching on us next? Shouldn't we take action now, before the evil of Auden Ironbound arrives on our shores?"

Fiona cast a sideways glance at her mother, hoping that she hadn't overstepped her bounds. The proud smile on Queen Leana's face gave Fiona hope.

An instant later, though, that hope fizzled into nothingness.

Some of the *selkies*—Fiona's eyes started to water, blurring her vision and keeping her from knowing how many—were *laughing*.

"Bravo!" Neely said, clapping as she chuckled. "An impassioned speech. You are your mother's daughter, Princess."

"A dear youngling you have there, my queen," Maeve said, smiling indulgently. "You'll do well, Princess, under your mother's tutelage. You have much to learn."

"She's barely gotten her flippers wet!" Erynn jeered.

"B-but . . . ," Fiona stammered.

"No shame in being inexperienced," Maeve said. "I'm sure we all look forward to what you'll be capable of achieving once you've learned the history of our kind."

"And the truth about the land-Changers," Erynn muttered, low enough that Fiona wasn't sure that anyone else had heard her.

Queen Leana rose. "Council is adjourned," she announced, turning the hourglass one last time. "We will meet next month; sooner, if circumstances demand. Go with the wind; go with the tide; go with grace."

"May it be," the others chorused, but not Fiona. She was already hurrying out of the cave, staring down so that no one could see how her face burned with anger and embarrassment.

Why did I come here? she wondered wildly. *Didn't they know? Didn't Ms. Therian and Mr. Kimura and the others know how the* selkies *would react?*

Mom had said that the *selkies* were a proud people, but Fiona hadn't seen any evidence of that. Their pride was buried so deeply under arrogance and ignorance that they couldn't even understand the danger that was right before them.

As Fiona stormed to the other side of the beach, she couldn't help but think back to the woman her father had reminisced about yesterday morning. Leana had been wild and carefree when she and Fiona's dad had first met, but now that Fiona had a chance to be with her mom, she realized that being queen had changed her. Compared to the whimsical *selkie* storyteller she'd heard about, Queen Leana was exceedingly practical, bound by the rules and prejudices of the *selkies*. She'd be no help to the other Changers.

Fiona tugged her cloak across her shoulders. The full moon blazed overhead. She had to get home, she had to get back to Willow Cove, back to the First Four. Auden Ironbound would attack in the morning; there wasn't much time. . . .

Fiona was certain of one thing, though. She knew where her allegiances lay. The other *selkies* might not care about the fate of the land-Changers, but Fiona did. She would fight side by side with them until the bitter end, no matter what.

"Fiona. Wait."

Mom's voice carried clearly across the sand. Fiona stopped, but she didn't turn around. A few moments later, she felt Mom's gentle hand rest on her shoulder.

"We need to talk," Mom said. "Come with me."

Fiona hesitated. *Talk? We talked and talked—and accomplished nothing,* she thought. *The time for talking is done. It's action that matters now.*

But as Mom began walking toward the ocean, Fiona had a strange, prickling feeling inside. It told her that she should listen. It told her that she should follow.

By the time Fiona caught up with her mother, they had both transformed. Fiona dove into the crystal water alongside her mom. This time, though, they didn't swim farther out to sea. Instead, Mom took a sharp turn and dove down, down, down . . . until they were swimming through the darkest depths, with no light from the moon or the stars to show the way.

We're swimming under the Isles of Saorsie, Fiona thought suddenly, and the thought made her realize that whatever Mom wanted to tell her—whatever she had to say—was important enough that they had to be completely and utterly alone.

After several minutes Fiona realized that she could see, vaguely, the outline of Mom swimming before her. *There's light,* she thought.

But where was it coming from?

At last, Mom and Fiona surfaced. Fiona took a deep, lung-stretching breath. They were in some sort of underground cavern; glittering stalactites hung from the ceiling as the salt water lapped against the sides of the cave. Fiona still couldn't tell where the light was coming from, though. Bluish and wavering, it was simultaneously soothing and unsettling.

We are in a sacred space.

Mom's voice rang through Fiona's head.

This is the Chamber of the Queens, Mom continued. *Our ancestors have long taken refuge in this hallowed space during times of turmoil and trouble. Before we begin, though, I must ask that you not judge the council too harshly.*

For Fiona, that was the last straw.

She pulled herself out of the water and let her *selkie* cloak slip off her shoulders. "I mustn't judge *them*?" she asked, her voice echoing through the stony cave. "Why didn't you tell *them* not to judge *me*? Just because I'm young doesn't mean my ideas don't matter! Just because I'm young doesn't mean that I don't matter!"

Mom transformed too. "I agree," she said evenly. "And they would too, if they weren't blinded by age and the self-satisfaction of considering themselves very, very wise."

"You—you agree? With me?" Fiona asked, struggling to understand.

"The council is, on the whole, an impressive and important group of *selkie* elders," her mother explained. "That does not, however, mean that they are infallible. Do you want to know a secret?"

Fiona nodded.

"I suspect the threat of Auden Ironbound's attack is so terrifying that many of them are in a deep state of denial," Mom confided. "But I'm not."

"You're worried?" asked Fiona.

"Beings like Auden Ironbound can only be overcome through unity," Mom told her. "And right now, the Changers—including the *selkies*—are anything but unified."

"You have to convince them," Fiona said. "You have to make them understand—"

"It was the elders' inflexibility that kept me away from my kind for so long," Mom told her. "But after I took my place as their queen, I realized something. Their hearts are true. They just need a push in the right direction, and they will gladly, selflessly, do the right thing."

"So *push* them!" Fiona exclaimed.

Mom shook her head, a strange smile on her face. "That's not my part to play in this," she said. "It's yours."

"I can't," Fiona said. "You saw. I tried and failed."

Mom placed her finger on Fiona's lips to silence her. "Aren't you wondering why I've brought you here, to the sacred heart of our ancestral home?"

"Of course I am," Fiona whispered. "Why?"

"Because," Mom said, "this is the only place where you can earn the Queen's Song."

One of the selkie songs! Fiona thought eagerly. At last, one of her deepest wishes was about to come true. "You'll teach it to me?" she said.

"I didn't say '*learn*,'" she corrected Fiona. "I said '*earn*.'"

Fiona hesitated with confusion.

"The Queen's Song is precious to our kind," Mom explained. "I alone know it. But if you prove yourself to be wise, strong, and courageous, then you too will carry it in your heart—no matter where you go, no matter what may happen."

"What does it do?" asked Fiona.

"It binds all magic, rendering it useless," Mom replied. "You must use it to save the Changers from Auden Ironbound. I fear they are woefully unprepared for his attack, defenseless in the face of his new scheme. But most importantly, the Queen's Song will protect you. For once you know it, the Horn of Power will have no effect on you."

"You don't need to worry about that," she said. "The Horn of Power doesn't work on younglings. That's how we were able to fight Auden Ironbound before, even after the adult Changers fell under its spell."

Fiona thought the news would make her mother feel better, but the queen's expression only grew more troubled. "They don't know?" she whispered.

"Don't know what?" asked Fiona.

"The horn's repair didn't just fix it," Mom explained. "It strengthened it too. Now the Horn of Power will enchant younglings as well."

Chapter 10
THE TRIAL

"How did I miss this?" Fiona gasped. "*That's* why the warlocks were kidnapping younglings instead of adults! *That's* why they stole their powers to repair it!"

"Yes," Mom said.

"They're in danger—all of them!" Fiona said. She grabbed her mother's hands. "Please, Mom, you've got to come with me, back to Willow Cove. We have to warn them. The Queen's Song—"

"Will be yours—"

"No!" Fiona cried. "No, it's too important, the stakes are too high, it has to be you! *Please*, Mom, *please*! What if—what if I fail?"

"You won't."

"But what if I do?"

"Fiona."

For the first time since their reunion, Mom's voice rang out with such firmness that it caught Fiona by surprise. She took Fiona's face in her hands. "You must calm yourself," Mom told her. "I know it's scary, but this was always your destiny. You were born for this battle."

Fiona stared into her mother's eyes for a long moment and knew that there was nothing she could say to change the queen's mind.

"Come," Mom said. "We have no time to lose."

Mom led Fiona to a small opening in the cave wall. "You will face three trials. Each one will reveal a different part of the Queen's Song," she said. "Good luck, and I'll see you on the other side."

"Wait," Fiona said urgently. "Aren't you coming with me?"

Something flickered across Mom's face then—a strange expression of foreboding, as chilling as a cloud covering the sun. "I can't," she said. "But . . . you will not be alone."

"I—"

Mom tucked Fiona's *selkie* cloak across her shoulders and kissed her forehead. Then, without another word, she transformed and dove back into the inky waters.

Fiona took a deep breath and looked around. Mom had said she wouldn't be alone, but that was exactly how she felt.

Let's get started, Fiona thought, trying to psych herself up. She'd never minded tests before.

Then again, she'd never had to take a test quite like this.

Fiona walked through the narrow passageway until she reached another underground chamber. This one was high and dry, and the moment Fiona entered it, the tunnel behind her sealed itself. She looked around and realized that she was in a closed stone cavern like the one she was in during the council meeting. The walls glimmered with flecks of mica and mineral deposits; rocks covered the floor. There wasn't a passageway or opening anywhere.

Trapped.

The word entered Fiona's mind without warning; just thinking it caused her heart to beat a little faster. She immediately tried to calm herself down. *Mom wouldn't send me off to some abandoned cavern with no escape,* Fiona thought firmly. *There's a way out of here. I just have to find it.*

Suddenly, Fiona's eyes widened. *Maybe that's the first test!* she realized. And with that thought, a glowing verse appeared on the cave wall.

> *Walls and stones, stacks of bones*
> *Are anchors, to be sure.*
> *Use your mind, break the bind,*
> *With wits both true and pure.*

"It's a riddle," Fiona said aloud. That wasn't too bad. She enjoyed solving riddles and puzzles. But she glanced around at the piles of rocks in the cavern and wondered, with a sickish feeling, if there might be bones—or something even worse—beneath them.

Is this a burial chamber for selkie *queens?* Fiona thought. *No. Don't think about it. Think about getting out of here.*

She paced the walls of the chamber, examining each one for any cracks. They all seemed solid—and yet, Fiona knew that couldn't be true, because there'd been an entrance to this room. She'd managed to get *in*; now she had to find a way *out*.

Think, think, think, Fiona told herself. *The riddle . . . It must be a clue. . . .*

She stared at the words again, frowning in concentration. *Forget about the stones and bones,* she thought. *The focus here is on the mind. . . . Mind . . . mind over matter. . . .*

Fiona sat down and cleared her mind. She let her eyes go out of focus; the cave walls blurred until all she could see was a smattering of shining spots where the mica reflected the light. They were all uneven; there was no pattern she could detect until . . .

Was that the shape of a doorway?

It was hard to tell.

Fiona walked across the cavern and felt the rough stone wall with her hand. It was cold and hard; completely solid—

Or was it?

Use your mind, break the bind . . . , Fiona thought. *If I truly believed that this was a passageway—if I charged at it . . .*

Fiona made a fist, pulled back her arm, and punched the wall as hard as she could.

Then she cried out—not in pain but in complete

and utter shock. Her hand disappeared into the stone as her arm plunged through the rock. It was very cold—and deeply unsettling—but Fiona knew what she had to do. With a deep breath, she pushed the rest of her body into the rockface and pulled herself through it to the other side.

Fiona looked around. She was in another chamber now; this one was lit with a soft blue light that emanated from a deep body of water.

A series of haunting notes began to ricochet off the water before her.

The Queen's Song, Fiona thought.

The notes faded into nothingness, but Fiona already had them in her heart. She could feel it, just as she could feel that was only the start of the song. She stepped forward, renewed and recharged, eager to learn the rest.

And there was another riddle on the wall;

> *Not faint nor meek; 'tis strength queens seek—*
> *Not of body nor of mind.*
> *But don't be slow in depths below;*
> *You'll need the strength you'll find.*

It *figures there'd be some sort of swimming trial*, Fiona

thought. She transformed and dove into the water without giving it a second thought.

That was a mistake.

Fiona had barely sunk below the surface when she suddenly felt a creeping chill down her spine. That feeling, more than anything else, told Fiona that she wasn't alone. *Just like Mom warned me*, Fiona thought. Then she shook her head. *Not warned me*—promised *me.*

A pair of glowing eyes.

Then another.

And another.

Fiona steeled herself. She wasn't alone at all . . . but the creatures who suddenly surrounded her on all sides were definitely not human.

In fact, they weren't even alive.

Fiona was surrounded by glowing *selkies. Ghost* selkies, she realized, so transparent that she could see water currents pass right through them. Each one wore a tiara, and that's when Fiona understood that they weren't just *selkie* ghosts.

They were the ghosts of *selkie* queens.

Their eyes were hollow, haunting, and they looked

at Fiona as if they wanted something from her—but what?

She didn't know, and she didn't want to find out.

With a fast flick of her hind flipper, Fiona darted through the water. She was confident in her swimming abilities, confident that she could get away from the ghost queens.

That was another mistake.

Fleeing only enraged them. Fiona could feel their anger pulsing through the water like sound waves, and she didn't have to turn around to know that they were following her.

Worse, they were *gaining* on her.

A surge of panic welled in Fiona, choking her as she struggled to swim even faster. The underground sea narrowed into a tight channel—almost impossible to navigate, with a low ceiling and sharp turns. But Fiona had to get away; she had to get away *fast*—

Wham!

Fiona was so preoccupied with her worries that she didn't even realize she'd reached a dead end. At some point that narrow strait had twisted into an underwater labyrinth—and now she was stuck. Solid stone walls surrounded her on three sides; in a desperate attempt to escape, Fiona tried to shove her flipper through them, but no luck; they were rock-solid.

And the fourth side? That's where the army of ghost queens approached, bearing down on Fiona in steady, silent judgment.

Fiona's lungs pulsed with pain. She would need oxygen soon; she would *have* to get out of this maze and breach the surface of the water. The thought of taking a deep breath of pure, cool air made her want to cry. She'd come so far—so very, very far—and for what? To become a *selkie* ghost like these menacing queens?

The ghost queens swam toward her, above her, under her, their spindly fingers reaching, getting closer. . . .

What do you want?

The words sprang from Fiona's mind fully formed—not just a question, but an accusation. She was angry, and it felt surprisingly good.

The ghost queens shimmered, paused, and were still.

The words of the riddle came back to Fiona then:

'tis strength queens seek—/Not of body nor of mind. . . .

Strength of will! Fiona realized suddenly. *That's what the riddle left out—strength of will.*

Fiona pulled herself up to her full height; she fixed the ghost queens with an icy stare and thought, *Fall back and leave me alone.*

And they did.

One by one, the ghost queens dipped into a graceful bow as they moved backward, making a path for Fiona. She swam by them and saw each one duck her head in a gesture of respect.

Strength of will, Fiona marveled to herself. *It's so much more powerful than my fear.*

When at last Fiona had made her way out of the labyrinth and back to the surface, she realized that the ghost queens weren't chasing her anymore. They were accompanying her. They swam in a formation, row after glimmering row, and lifted their heads.

Then they began to sing.

Fiona recognized the first four notes immediately. *It's the Queen's Song!* she thought gleefully. To hear the ghost queens sing it was enchanting. She couldn't tear her eyes away from them as their tiaras began to glow, pulsing in time with the music.

There came a tremendous grinding noise, the sound of thousands of pounds of rock shifting, sliding. . . .

Fiona scrambled to get out of the way. . . .

An ancient staircase rose from the depths. Cracked and covered with algae, Fiona knew she was supposed to climb on. She changed back to her human form and leaped onto the lowest step. The staircase carried her up as the ghost queens bowed again and then faded into nothingness.

In moments, Fiona found herself locked within another stone chamber.

Three trials, she thought. *Three parts of the song. I'm almost finished!*

And that was a good thing, because Fiona was starting to feel very, very tired.

The final riddle illuminated itself on the wall.

> *When hope seems lost, at any cost,*
> *A queen will face this choice:*
> *To flee in fear, to shed a tear,*
> *Or raise her noble voice.*

Fiona read it again and then frowned. *That's not much of a puzzle,* she thought. *It's more like a motivational poster.*

Craaaaaaaaack.

The noise was so loud that it made Fiona jump. She glanced around wildly until she spotted a large crack snaking up a stone wall.

The chamber trembled.

Then, one by one, rocks began to fall. The chamber was crumbling, and if Fiona didn't find a way out, she would surely be crushed.

Think. Think. Think, she told herself, keeping close watch on the ceiling so she could dodge any stones that threatened to fall on her. A *test for wisdom, a test for strength—*

"Ahhhh!" Fiona screamed, jumping to the side as a boulder plummeted toward her. It was a close call—too close.

She tried to focus, but it was almost impossible with the thunderous crash of rocks falling all around her. Fiona was terrified. And yet she knew in her heart that there *had* to be a way out.

Now all she had to do was find it.

Fiona spoke the words of the riddle aloud. Somehow, hearing them made all the difference.

"Voice," she said, her voice barely audible amid the sound of falling rocks. "Of course."

Then she took a deep breath and began to sing the Queen's Song. She didn't know all of it, but she knew enough—at least, Fiona *hoped* she knew enough.

Yet the rocks kept plummeting. Fiona was getting desperate. She knew now why the stone staircase was so pitted. If one of those rocks hit *her*—

Raise your voice.

Fiona wasn't sure what made those words pop into her mind. Holding on to the staircase for support—it seemed to be getting more wobbly by the second—she stared at the riddle again. "Am I supposed to sing louder?" she asked.

There was no answer, of course.

Fiona hesitated. She'd never sung loudly before in her entire life. Whenever she sang, it was under her breath, humming as she did the dishes or walked along the beach. Singing loud would feel as strange and unfamiliar to her as waking up with a second head.

But the rocks were coming faster now . . . falling harder . . .

Fiona reached deep down inside herself, opened her mouth, and sang with all her heart. Her voice had never been louder; it filled the air with a power that Fiona had never even imagined she might possess. The staircase stopped shaking; the rocks stopped crumbling. It was as if the stony chamber itself had paused to listen.

I'm singing the Queen's Song! Fiona thought in delight.

When she reached the end of the second verse, the staircase began to move upward again, strong and steady once more. An opening in the ceiling appeared; Fiona looked up and saw the stars. The staircase brought her up until she was on the surface of the Isles of Saorsie again.

And Mom was waiting for her.

"Well done, my girl," Mom whispered as she kissed Fiona's forehead. "You've earned the Queen's Song." Then she took Fiona's hands and began to sing, teaching Fiona the third and final part.

As Mom sang, her tiara began to glow, just like the ghost *selkies. No, wait,* Fiona thought. *It isn't the tiara that's glowing.* An elaborate runic symbol appeared on Mom's forehead, gleaming with a warm light that grew brighter with every note she sang.

It was the most breathtaking magic Fiona had ever seen.

With her eyes still closed, Queen Leana lifted her arm into the air and pressed a fingertip to Fiona's forehead. Fiona's forehead began to burn like she had a fever. She didn't need a mirror to know that her skin now had a glowing rune on it too.

Fiona opened her mouth and sang to the stars. Two voices were raised in one song, lifting the melody into the fathomless night. It was so beautiful—the most beautiful thing Fiona had ever heard. . . .

Then the song came to its end, and the last note hung in the air before fading away. In the silence that followed, Fiona took a deep breath.

"You're ready," Mom finally said. "It's time to go."

"I don't want to leave you," Fiona said in a small voice.

"You must," Mom replied. "You have a long swim ahead of you, and Auden Ironbound approaches. I can feel it. And . . ."

"And what?" Fiona asked after her mom's voice trailed off.

"He's not alone."

Fiona's breath caught in her throat, which suddenly felt tight and swollen. She nodded, not trusting herself to speak, as she stood up and clutched the *selkie* cloak across her shoulders.

"Wait," Mom said urgently. "When you sing, Fiona, you must sing with conviction to your intended target. You have to mean it, really mean it; every note must come from your heart. Do you understand? This is very important—perhaps the most important part of all. . . ."

"I understand," she said.

Fiona would have liked to linger. She wanted one more minute, one more hug, one more word of reassurance or advice.

Instead, Fiona spun around, transformed, and disappeared beneath the churning waves.

Chapter 11
THE RING OF TEZCATLIPOCA

"Go."

After hours of silence, Mr. Kimura's voice made everyone—Yara, Sefu, Tía Rosa, Darren, and Gabriella—jump. His eyes were still closed; in fact, he hadn't moved a muscle since he'd entered a deep, meditative trance, trying to understand the curse that had taken hold of Mack.

"You found out what it is?" Ms. Therian asked in a high, anxious voice. *The Compendium* lay open in her lap; she'd been poring over it for hours.

"No," Mr. Kimura replied, keeping his eyes shut. "It's Fiona."

Oh, no, Gabriella worried. *What's happened to her?*

"She's on her way home," Mr. Kimura continued. "She knows . . . something. Meet her on the shore. Guard her and guide her to safety."

Yara and Sefu rose at the same time and slipped from the room without a word.

"And her mom?" asked Gabriella. "Is the queen with Fiona?"

Mr. Kimura shook his head. "Fiona swims alone, without Queen Leana or the other *selkies*, against the tide."

Then Mr. Kimura opened his eyes and looked directly at Ms. Therian. "It's time."

She nodded, just once, as if what Mr. Kimura had said made sense. Gabriella glanced at Darren and wondered if he was as frustrated as she felt. *It's like they're speaking in code*, she thought in annoyance. *I wish they'd clue the rest of us in.*

Gabriella was about to ask Mr. Kimura what he meant when his voice suddenly sounded in her head. She looked at him, startled. His lips weren't moving. That's when she realized that he wasn't speaking at all.

He was sending a message—to every Changer in the world.

My friends, Mr. Kimura began. *The time has come to take shelter from the storm. Report to the nearest Harbor at once, and you will have full protection against Auden Ironbound.*

The silence when he finished was overwhelming.

"That's it, then?" Gabriella finally asked. "We're all just going to hide now?"

"What if the bad Changers slip into the Harbors?" Darren added. "They could attack from the inside."

Mr. Kimura fixed them both with his even, unflinching stare. "The Harbors were enchanted by Fiona's mother before the *selkies* split from our nation; they guard against anything and anyone—magic or Changer—with malevolent intentions, and they can withstand any spell, including the Horn's call. But Auden will eventually find the Harbors. That many magical beings close together will leave a trace . . . and the supplies stockpiled there won't last more than a few months. The most important thing for now is that we prevent Auden's army from growing and reaping more devastation," he said. "As for tomorrow, I have no intention of hiding. I have an obligation to protect my people."

"Surely you didn't forget about our plan B," said Ms. Therian.

"What *is* plan B?" asked Darren. "Gabriella and I don't know anything about it."

"After Auden Ironbound's announcement, we began investigating magical objects," Ms. Therian told them. "We thought that perhaps, somewhere in the wide world, there might be one with the ability to defeat the Horn of Power."

Hope unfurled in Gabriella's heart. "And did you find one?" she asked eagerly.

"Not quite," Mr. Kimura replied. "But we found something that we believe will help. The Ring of Tezcatlipoca."

Mr. Kimura took The Compendium from Ms. Therian and flipped through the pages until he found a certain entry. "Here," he said, passing the book to Darren.

Gabriella craned her neck to read along with Darren.

"'The Ring of Tezcatlipoca,'" Darren began. "'An ancient artifact of obsidian and gold, it endows the wearer with intense spiritual strength, such that it resists mind control spells or objects. Though the ring bears no other defenses, it is nevertheless a coveted and unusual object, much desired by anyone about to engage in battle.'"

Darren glanced up from the page. "Let me get this straight," he said. "If you wear the ring, the Horn of Power will have no effect on you?"

Mr. Kimura nodded. "That is our hope," he said.

"When can we get it?" asked Gabriella.

Tía Rosa smiled coyly. "I had my own mission last night—to the underground caverns at the ruins in Teopanzolco," she said, a hint of pride in her voice. She held out her hand to reveal a flash of gold. The Ring of Tezcatlipoca was stunning, made of pure gold, with an elaborate carving of a man's face on the front, and beautiful designs along the band. A horizontal streak of obsidian ran across the center of the man's face.

"This is incredible!" Darren exclaimed. "We have the ring! We can beat Auden Ironbound now! How come this isn't plan A?"

"The ring is untested against the Horn of Power," Mr. Kimura cautioned. "We have no idea if it will work. That is why the Ring of Tezcatlipoca is our last resort."

Which means they've lost confidence in our other options, Gabriella thought. That made sense, she supposed—especially now that they knew Fiona had been unable to persuade the *selkies* to join them.

Mr. Kimura rose slowly, as if his bones ached. "I will take the ring and meet Auden Ironbound on the beach," he said. "If I can defeat Auden and his followers, the curse on Mack should be broken."

"We'll come with you," Darren said.

"No," Mr. Kimura replied.

Gabriella and Darren both started talking at once, until Tía Rosa hissed at them to hush.

"I will not knowingly put you in danger," Mr. Kimura continued.

"But we're immune to the Horn of Power," Gabriella argued. "It can't affect us."

"True, but we don't know what else Auden Ironbound is planning," Mr. Kimura explained. "Your safety is of the utmost importance. This is especially critical *because* you are unaffected by the horn. If I should fail—if Willow Cove falls to Auden Ironbound and his army—"

A sharp knock interrupted Mr. Kimura. He

exchanged a wordless glance with Ms. Therian, who nodded in response.

Mr. Kimura pushed *The Compendium* into Gabriella's arms and then pulled a fake book from the bookshelf, out of which he drew Circe's Compass from a secret compartment. The ancient relic could point the way to other Changers. He handed it to Darren.

"I don't understand," Gabriella said. "Why are you giving these to us?"

"Listen, both of you," Mr. Kimura said urgently. "If the First Four should fall to Auden Ironbound, the two of you, along with Mack and Fiona, are the new First Four. You'll need to leave Willow Cove quickly."

Gabriella shifted her stance. "But—"

"*Quickly,*" Mr. Kimura repeated. "By that time, Auden Ironbound will be nearly unstoppable. He will seek to capture as many Changers as possible. The nearest active Harbor is south of here, down along the coast; that will likely be his next stop. You both go north and then east, to Oak Town. Travel by night. Do you understand?"

Gabriella couldn't believe what she was hearing. She looked over to her aunt to be sure that she was understanding Mr. Kimura correctly. To her shock, Tía Rosa's eyes were wide. *Could she really be afraid?* Gabriella wondered. In that moment, Gabriella realized that the only thing worse than her own fears was seeing her brave aunt, the heroic Emerald Wildcat, preparing for the worst. *We have to be ready for anything*, Gabriella reminded herself as she tried to conquer her panic.

"There is another Harbor in Oak Town," Mr. Kimura continued. "Ask *The Compendium*, and it will lead you there. The Harbor is defunct now, but there are still supplies. Since it's just the four of you, Leana's enchantments on the Harbor will conceal your location from Auden. Access the emergency protocols in its library when you get there. "

"What about you?" Gabriella asked, turning to Tía Rosa. "Where will you be? And the rest of the First Four?"

"We'll be at the Willow Cove Harbor with all the Changers who've sought the First Four's protection," Tía Rosa explained. "As soon as I have a chance, I'll come find you. I swear it."

"Why can't we go to the base with you?" asked Gabriella, urging herself not to cry.

"You need to escape while you can," Tía Rosa told

her. "If Auden Ironbound finds the bases, everyone there will be trapped. He'll wait until our supplies run out and then capture us."

Gabriella locked eyes with her aunt and understood then exactly what she was trying to tell her: this could be the last time they would ever see each other. "Okay," she said, taking a final shuddering breath as she tried to process everything that was happening.

"Rosa, please take the younglings to their homes," Mr. Kimura said.

"Why? What's going on?" Gabriella asked.

"The Willow Cove Harbor is beneath the house," Mr. Kimura explained. "We are in for a long night, and you both need your rest for what may come. Please, be awake by dawn—and be ready to take action."

"We will," Gabriella promised—though in her heart, she wondered how she and Darren could ever hope to escape if Mr. Kimura failed.

When Gabriella stepped outside, she could hardly believe her eyes: There was a line of Changers stretching down the path, all the way into the street; more and more arrived by the second. *Mr. Kimura just made that announcement,* she marveled. *They got here so fast.*

"Aren't your neighbors going to notice this?" Darren asked Mr. Kimura. "What if someone calls the police?"

"No need to worry," Mr. Kimura replied calmly. "Ordinary people can't see them. It's one of the many enchantments we've placed on this street."

Then, to Gabriella's surprise, Mr. Kimura put one hand on her shoulder and the other on Darren's. "Whatever may come, you are both ready to face it," he said. "Go. Be safe, be strong for our people."

"Thank you," Gabriella said. Then she followed Tía Rosa to the car.

They dropped off Darren and then continued home in a heavy, uncomfortable silence, thick with dread and fear. Gabriella's house was only a few minutes away, but she found herself wishing that the drive would stretch on for hours. All too soon, they arrived; blinking back tears, Gabriella threw her arms around her aunt's neck and hugged her tight.

"Have faith, *mija,*" Tía Rosa whispered. "The time before the battle—the waiting, the worrying—is the worst of all. It won't be much longer now."

"I love you," Gabriella replied. It was all she could manage to say.

"I love you, too. And I'll see you soon," Tía Rosa promised.

As Gabriella walked up the path to her front door, she didn't have to turn around and look to know that Tía Rosa was watching to make sure she made it in safely. Gabriella was suddenly so tired that she didn't even bother to brush her teeth, but instead went straight to her bedroom, where she set her alarm for four o'clock in the morning. Mr. Kimura wanted them ready before dawn, and Gabriella wasn't going to let him down.

She placed The Compendium on her bedside table, right next to her phone. Somehow Gabriella felt better about everything with The Compendium nearby. She closed her eyes but knew that it was going to take a while for all the thoughts that were running through her head to quiet. Still, soon enough, she found her eyelids feeling heavier and heavier. . . .

BANG!

Gabriella jerked up, her heart thundering in her

chest. Had the battle already begun? Was that an explosion? A warning, perhaps?

Or something even worse?

Her hand was shaking as she reached for the lamp on her bedside table. Part of her hated to turn it on, but it was still too dark to see; dawn had not yet arrived. *Just turn it on,* Gabriella scolded herself. *You're not some baby who's afraid of the dark.*

Click.

The soft glow of the lamp provided just enough light for Gabriella to figure out what had happened: somehow, *The Compendium* had fallen to the floor, open.

As Gabriella picked up the book, the words on the page seemed to swim across it, letters tumbling as they rearranged themselves.

The Ring of Tezcatlipoca

An ancient artifact forged from obsidian and gold, it endows the wearer with intense spiritual strength, such that it resists mind control spells or objects. Though the ring bears no other defenses, it is nevertheless a coveted and unusual object, much desired by anyone about to engage in battle. However, those who seek its Protection would be Wise to understand that the Ring is only effective for those of Aztec Blood.

Hold up, Gabriella realized. She was certain the last line hadn't been there before. She'd been reading along over Darren's shoulder. Surely she would've noticed a condition like that—or someone else would've—

Gabriella's thoughts swirled wildly. *This says—this says that the ring will only work on someone with Aztec blood,* she thought. *Which means that Mr. Kimura won't be protected at all! He probably doesn't even know. Those words appeared for* me, *not him or Darren—*

Gabriella didn't understand it, she couldn't explain it, but somehow the same power that made the Ring of Tezcatlipoca only work for those with Aztec blood meant that only they could learn its true secrets . . . and its limitations.

As if in a dream, she reached for her phone and texted Darren as fast as she could.

> Meet me at the beach. Mr. Kimura is in danger!

Chapter 12
HOMECOMING

Swim. Swim. Swim.

It was a one-word mantra, repeating in Fiona's brain until the word itself no longer had any meaning.

Swim. Swim. Swim.

It was the hardest thing she'd ever done—and yet a thousand times better than the alternative. To succumb, to surrender, to *sink.*

No, Fiona promised herself. *Never.*

Swim. Swim. Swim.

How long had she been at it now? An hour? A day? A year? It seemed impossible to know. Time had no meaning in the murky depths of the ocean, where the light of the stars and the moon disappeared into nothingness. There was a time when "nothingness" was the last word that Fiona ever would've used to describe the vast oceans, teeming with life of all sorts, but that was before. After the longest night, unable to see anything, swimming all alone—

Suddenly, Fiona felt a strange tingling along her spine.

Was she all alone?

Fiona wasn't sure anymore.

There's magic in the water, she realized. A figure was moving toward her; the current now had a faint, almost phosphorescent, glow as it parted, letting the creature—a dolphin, perhaps—glide through effortlessly. How Fiona envied that; after swimming as quickly as she could for so long, each stroke felt like agony to her.

Even through the pain and exhaustion, though, Fiona clearly remembered Ms. Therian's warning to flee from any Changer who approached her in the water. *They've come to attack,* Fiona thought in desperation, somehow managing to find a last burst of strength as she swam furiously away from what she could now sense was an *encantado.*

Then a familiar voice called her name.

Fiona! Wait! Yara cried in Fiona's mind. *Sefu and I have been searching for you for hours!*

Yara! Fiona cried. *How did you find me?*

It hasn't been easy. We feared the worst, Yara told her. *Come, we've got to get you back to shore. Sefu is waiting.*

Is it far? Fiona asked, hating the weakness that had begun to overpower her. *I'm so tired. Where are we?*

The dolphin gently nudged Fiona with her snout. *Not too far, Fiona. Come on. You can do it. I'm here with you. I'll help. Let me light the way.*

Fiona was too tired to even wonder how Yara managed to cast an ethereal glow through the water, but she appreciated that small light more than she could say.

Say—

Someone was saying something—

It was so hard to concentrate when all she wanted to do was *sleep*—

Fiona, Yara's voice cut through her thoughts. *Stay with me. Did you find your mother—the queen? What happened?*

Fiona shook her head. *She wouldn't come with me,* she admitted. *The selkie council voted for neutrality. I failed.*

No! *Never say that,* Yara exclaimed. *All we asked was that you try. And you did. It was always a long shot, Fiona, you know that. Akira has a plan, so there's a chance. . . .*

Fiona could tell that Yara was still talking, but it was hard to understand her words. The waves rocked her back and forth, back and forth; she was cradled by them. *I'll just close my eyes for a moment,* she thought. *Yara is here. She'll take care of everything.*

Fiona remembered being rocked like this, long ago, in her mother's arms. How her mother would hold her; how her mother would sing—

Sing.

Half asleep, slipping deeper into unconsciousness every moment, Fiona tried to pull herself back to reality. Yara's sharp voice helped. *Fiona! You have to stay alert! I can help, but I can't do this for you!*

Fiona could tell Yara wasn't mad, just worried—there was so much to worry about, so much to remember . . .

I remember, Fiona thought. Her eyes fluttered open. *Yara—I passed the trials. I know the Queen's Song.*

Yara gasped. *No,* she said, as if she couldn't believe it was true. *Oh, Fiona! Don't you know what this means?*

It has to be me, Fiona told her. *I have the weapon to stop Auden Ironbound's magic. And there's something else, too. . . .*

What? Yara asked urgently. *What?*

Fiona struggled to remember through the fog of her exhaustion. *The Horn of Power,* she began. *It's— stronger now. Since the repair. Younglings won't be immune anymore.*

For an instant Yara stopped swimming, trying to understand. *Are you saying—*

But Fiona never learned what Yara was about to ask. At that moment a massive force slammed into Yara, tossing her aside like a toy.

Fiona watched in horror as a terrible realization dawned on her.

It was a shark!

Not just any shark, though; she felt a trace of magic. Fiona was certain it was a Changer. Another betrayer, willing to abandon all that was good and right in the world to align with Auden.

Yara plunged back into the water, hitting the surface so hard that a massive wave washed over Fiona. The shark circled back, its cruel teeth glinting.

Keep swimming, Fiona, Yara's voice rang through Fiona's head. *You're almost there. You must get back to shore as fast as you can.*

How could Fiona leave Yara all alone in the churning waters, pursued by the bloodthirsty shark?

Go! Now! Yara ordered her, and then breached the surface in a tall, graceful arc.

She's leading the shark Changer away from me—and away from the shore, Fiona realized.

This was Fiona's chance.

She reached deep inside herself for one last burst of energy and pushed forward. She honestly didn't know if she could make it, but the ocean itself seemed to sense her need, and the tide shifted. Fiona relaxed and let it carry her closer, closer, closer. . . .

Her flippers brushed against the ocean floor. . . .

Fiona pulled herself onto the beach and rolled over, trying to catch her breath. There were five figures silhouetted against the sky, arguing frantically.

The sky—Fiona squinted up at it. Not night, not yet day, but somewhere in between. The sun seemed to be struggling to rise, leaving a sickly greenish-yellow cast to the horizon. Dawn would soon arrive—and so would Auden Ironbound.

"Fiona!"

Gabriella's voice carried over the sound of the wind and the waves.

Fiona shrugged off her *selkie* cloak and tried to pull herself up, but her exhausted muscles trembled, threatening to give out. Gabriella was by her side in an instant.

"Steady, steady," Gabriella said. "I've got you. Just take it one step at a time."

Gabriella helped Fiona up the beach toward Mr. Kimura, Sefu, Ms. Therian, and Darren. *Someone's missing,* Fiona thought, but her mind was so bleary it took a moment to figure out who.

"Mack," she said. "Where's Mack?"

"Later," Ms. Therian said shortly. "What happened?"

Fiona shook her head. "The *selkies* voted for neutrality," she said. "But I learned the Queen's Song. I know it."

"What's the Queen's Song?" asked Darren.

"It will stop Auden Ironbound's magic," Fiona explained. "And knowing it makes me immune to the Horn of Power, too."

"But we're already immune," Gabriella said.

"No," Fiona said, trying to explain through her exhaustion. "Not anymore."

Then her head, so heavy on her neck, fell forward as Fiona succumbed to sleep at last. There was a hand on her shoulder, shaking her.

"Let me sleep," she mumbled.

"Fiona, wake up, wake up!" Ms. Therian was saying. "We need you, Fiona. *Wake up!*"

Fiona forced her eyes open. "Sorry," she said. "What's going on?"

"You said that younglings are not immune to the horn anymore," Ms. Therian said urgently. "What did you mean by that?"

"My mom told me," Fiona replied. "Since it was repaired with the strength of younglings, they're no longer immune. That's why Auden Ironbound kidnapped Darren and the others."

A look of horror crossed Darren's face as he realized exactly what Fiona was saying. "I'm sorry—" he began.

"No," Mr. Kimura cut him off. "There's no need for that, and no time. Gabriella."

Mr. Kimura twisted a gleaming gold ring off his finger. His hand was steady as he held out the ring to her. Fiona was too tired to wonder about it.

"There's no time to summon Rosa. You are our only hope of forestalling Auden Ironbound's attack," Mr. Kimura told Gabriella. "Whatever it takes, you *must* delay him long enough for Fiona to finish her song."

"Whatever it takes," she replied, nodding.

"And remember—"

Mr. Kimura stopped speaking abruptly; something in the distance had captured his attention. When Fiona turned around to see, adrenaline surged through her veins.

Against a bloodred sky, Auden Ironbound stood, with his army in perfect formation behind him. From this distance, Fiona couldn't tell if they were Changers or warlocks—not that it mattered. Because every last one of them was ready to fight.

Auden Ironbound raised the Horn of Power, which glinted in the light from the rising sun. Then he stepped forward, and in horrifying unison, the army began to march behind him, in lockstep.

They were coming.

All of a sudden, Fiona noticed that there was something else breaking through the crowd. She squinted her eyes, trying to get a closer look—it was a *kitsune* with two tails, his eyes glowing an eerie red—

Suddenly, Fiona gasped. "Mack!" she cried. "They've got Mack!"

"The curse?" Gabriella asked, looking to Mr. Kimura.

Mr. Kimura only nodded in response.

Gabriella's golden cat eyes were flashing with anger as she jammed the ring onto her finger. There was a faint crackling noise as a shimmering, magical force field surrounded her.

The ring, Fiona realized. *It's enchanted!*

"You have to go," Gabriella told the others. "I'll guard Fiona. Get back to the base as fast as you can, before it's too late."

Then came a sound both terrible and familiar: It resonated in their bodies, vibrating their very bones. The dreaded blast from the Horn of Power seemed to echo off the ocean itself.

It was already too late.

Chapter 13
The Queen's Song

Everything happened at the same time.

Gabriella transformed, the golden ring gleaming against her black fur as it cast a protective shield around her. Mr. Kimura's, Ms. Therian's, and Sefu's eyes all glowed red. They spun around and began marching toward Auden Ironbound's army, disappearing into its ranks. The horn had control of them—and there was nothing Fiona could do to reach them.

What about Darren? Fiona thought frantically.

Too late, Gabriella replied, gesturing at the sky with her paw. Fiona glanced up and saw Darren in his *impundulu* form, swooping overhead. Even from this distance, she could see that his eyes had turned red too. Just like that, their closest allies had become their enemies.

I don't understand, Fiona told Gabriella. *Why isn't the horn controlling you too?*

I'll explain later! Gabriella replied. *Just sing!*

Sing.

It sounded so easy when Gabriella said it like that. But Fiona was suddenly awash with dread. It was too much pressure, the stakes were too high. . . .

Every grain of sand trembled from the force of the army's march.

Fear overcame Fiona; she stumbled backward, wishing she could escape. But there was no escape; just the broad sea behind her. Already the rising tide was lapping at her feet.

The water.

Far beyond where the eye could see, Fiona's mother swam in these same waters. All those years she'd been out there, watching, waiting. It all came rushing back to her: swimming with Mom, the conch-lit shore of the Isles of Saorsie, the council, the trials . . .

The song.

The Queen's Song filled her heart; it flooded her veins; it even flowed into her lungs. That familiar warmth spread across her skin, and Fiona could picture the glowing rune appearing on her forehead.

She opened her mouth and sang.

Her voice was small but steady; the song sounded right, and that knowledge made Fiona more confident.

Just like you promised, Mom, she thought as the ancient melody escaped from her lips. *I'm singing the Queen's Song.*

The army kept approaching. Overhead, the clouds were gathering. They crackled with sparks, and Fiona knew that Darren was preparing to strike. To think he would use his lightning against her, against Gabriella . . .

No, she told herself. *That's not Darren. Darren would never do that. All of this is Auden Ironbound—all of this is his fault.*

Then, to Fiona's horror, she could clearly see Mr. Kimura, Ms. Therian, Sefu, and Mack among the warriors. As they came closer, Fiona could see their expressions more clearly. They looked eager to fight.

The sight made her feel sick, so sick that her song faltered—once, twice—

Gabriella's fur was standing on end as she swiped at the approaching army, her long claws glinting in the early-morning light. *Keep singing!* Gabriella urged Fiona. *I've got your back. . . . Don't think about them—close your eyes if you have to . . .*

Fiona followed Gabriella's advice, squeezing her eyes shut tight. At last, the crescendo—the last note carried on the ocean breeze like the pealing of a bell.

Fiona opened her eyes, hardly daring to hope that she had succeeded.

But the army was still moving. With every step they took, Fiona became more and more certain of one agonizing, undeniable truth: she had failed.

I don't understand, Fiona cried. *I sang it just like I did before! Why didn't it work?*

Try again! You can do it! Gabriella replied. The first wave of soldiers was just feet away now; there were too many of them for Gabriella to hold off by herself, but Fiona knew she would fight until the end.

If she won't give up, then neither will I, Fiona vowed. Then she began to sing again, though it was hard to keep singing when the danger was so great, bearing down on them from all sides. Fiona sang every last note her mother had taught her.

But the Queen's Song didn't even slow Auden Ironbound's approach.

Maybe this is it, Fiona thought numbly. *Maybe it was all for nothing.*

Sing louder!

Gabriella's command ripped through Fiona's brain, triggering something—something she should've remembered . . .

. . . you must sing with conviction. You have to mean it, really mean it; every note must come from your heart. . . .

And just like that, Fiona knew what she had to do—even though she had no idea how to begin.

How do I sing with conviction? she wondered. It was about more than just being loud, Fiona knew that much. But even finding more volume seemed insurmountable in the face of the approaching army.

Do it or die, Fiona suddenly thought. She reached down, down, down inside herself, past the fear and the exhaustion and the doubt until, at last, she discovered what she was looking for: her voice.

After all, it had been there all along, just waiting for Fiona to find it.

When Fiona opened her mouth to try again, she threw back her head and let the Queen's Song pour out, just as she had when she sang with her mother. No hesitation, no doubt. She sang to the sun and the stars; she sang to the ocean and the land; she sang to the *selkies*—who were far from her hearing—to the army that was bearing down upon her, but above all, to Auden Ironbound.

This time, it wasn't just Fiona's runic symbol that glowed, but the song itself: the music became corporeal, a pulsing, glimmering tendril that unfurled through the very air. The song, Fiona realized, was searching for something—for someone—

Auden Ironbound saw the song. He froze in mid-step, lifted the Horn of Power to his mouth, and blew that same long, threatening blast.

The Queen's Song, though, could not be drowned out, not even by the Horn of Power. Instead, it glowed brighter and brighter, until it hurt Fiona's eyes to watch it.

But she did not look away.

The song wrapped itself around Auden Ironbound's legs like a creeping vine or a poisonous snake; it enveloped him, looping up until, at last, it reached the Horn of Power. The horn started to glow too, just like the song, brighter and brighter until—

A blinding flash.

A sonic boom.

And then the whole world shook.

The horn exploded, shattering into billions of pieces, each no larger than a speck of dust. They rained onto the sand like a shower of ashes. Already the ocean breeze had started to scatter them across the whole, wide world; the Horn of Power was no more, obliterated for all time.

The air was torn by an agonizing scream. Auden Ironbound collapsed into a fit of rage, his defeat so bitter and so complete that there was nothing in the world he could do to recover. *He's lost his magic,* Fiona realized. *Not just the Horn of Power, but every last bit of magic he ever had.*

All around Auden Ironbound, a restless shift rippled through his army. The few Changers he'd managed to ensnare were waking from trances. Color returned to their eyes before they pursued the magic-users for revenge. Fiona could hear Mr. Kimura send a message to the Changers at the Harbors to head for the beach. A ferocious battle erupted in seconds, Changers against magic-users, but this time, at least, it would be a fair fight.

Now it's over, Fiona thought as the exhaustion overcame her, even worse than before. Her legs crumpled beneath her. She started to fall, but then, out of nowhere—

Strong arms caught her, held her tight.

"You did beautifully, my girl," Mom whispered into her ear.

EPILOGUE

"Mom," Fiona heard herself say, burying her face in her mother's shoulder. "You came."

"You know I've always been watching over you," Mom replied. "This battle was no exception. I couldn't be more proud of you, Fiona. And . . . it looks like I'm not the only one."

Fiona glanced up to see that she was surrounded—not by Auden Ironbound's army but by her own friends and allies. The First Four were there, even Yara, who was bruised and bleeding from her battle with the shark, but grinning so broadly that Fiona could tell she wasn't seriously hurt. Gabriella was there too, halfway transformed and not caring one bit. Darren had swooped down from above, and Mack ran to them, newly freed from what Fiona gathered had been a curse.

"Where's Dad?" Fiona asked. "He promised he'd be here."

"And he was, the whole night," Yara said. "He wouldn't leave, not for anything. We couldn't take the risk of him being present for the battle, so I had to enchant him for his own safety. Your father's home now, safe and sound."

Was that a glimmer of disappointment that crossed Mom's face? Did she, maybe, want to see Dad as much as Fiona did?

Fiona took hold of Yara's hand and squeezed it in gratitude. "Thank you for protecting my father," she said.

"Fiona! How did you even—" Mack began, so excited he was stumbling over his words. "Did you see what you did to the Horn of Power? You *destroyed* it. I mean, *wow*, that was some *serious* magic. You've gotta tell me how you did it!"

Fiona and her mother exchanged a knowing smile. "I don't know," she said. "It runs in the family, I guess."

"Well, it was *incredible*," Mack said.

"I had some help, you know," Fiona said, elbowing Gabriella. "I couldn't have done it by myself."

"Oh, stop," Gabriella said. "You were amazing."

"No, *you* were amazing," Fiona insisted.

"Hey," Darren spoke up as he pointed across the sand. "Check that out."

Everyone glanced over to see two Changers they knew, Miles Campagna and Ankur Iyer, wrapping Auden Ironbound in heavy algae-green chains. The evil warlock's head hung low in defeat.

"Thank you for the chains," Ms. Therian said to Queen Leana, bowing with respect.

The *Selkie* queen returned the bow. "Of course," she said. "I'm happy to provide them."

"Serves him right," Mack said with contempt as he watched Miles and Ankur drag Auden Ironbound away. "I can't believe one of his goons managed to curse me."

"Hey, at least you didn't get *kidnapped*," Darren said.

"He won't have the chance to do any of that again— to anyone," Ms. Therian said.

"An eternity in captivity will give him the chance

to consider his wrongdoings," added Mr. Kimura. He pulled Mack into a hug, as if he couldn't believe that his grandson was standing beside him, safe after all that had happened.

"The nightmare is over," Sefu declared. "Tonight, Changers around the world will celebrate."

"Speaking of Changers from around the world," Mack said, "did you guys see that golden *kitsune*?"

Everyone turned to look at him.

"A *golden kitsune*?" asked Gabriella, shaking her head.

"I didn't see one either," Darren added. "And I had a pretty good view from above."

"Too bad. She was incredible," Mack said. "I saw her tearing it up on the battlefield a few minutes ago. I've never seen fighting like that before. And she must've had seven tails!"

Mr. Kimura grabbed Mack's shoulders. "Seven tails?" he repeated in a strangled voice. "Did you say *seven*?"

"Well, I mean, I didn't really get a chance to count," Mack said. "Six or seven—something like that."

Sefu approached Mack too. "And you're sure she was golden?" he asked. "It wasn't just a trick of the light, perhaps? The early-morning sun shining off her coat?"

Mack shook his head. "Absolutely not," he replied. "I might not know exactly how many tails she had, but I am completely certain that she was golden. Her fur was beautiful."

Something's wrong, Fiona realized. She stared at the First Four, searching their faces for answers, longing for them to explain. Why did Mr. Kimura look so pale all of a sudden?

Sefu reached out and placed a steadying hand on his shoulder. "Well," he said, "it seems your old student has returned to you at last."

Mack fluffed couch pillows, folded newspapers for the recycling bin, and shook his head thinking about how steep his learning curve had been ever since he got the news in September. Powers begin to develop in a Changer's twelfth year, and he had learned what he was just before that started to happen. The first day of school immersed Mack and his friends in a new, secret, and sometimes confusing world.

Just as Mack, Gabriella, Darren, and Fiona were starting to learn how to handle their powers, a new warlock, Auden Ironbound, stole the Horn of Power and tried to recreate the terrible events that had transpired a thousand years ago. When Auden used the horn to take control of the First Four, it fell upon Mack and his friends to battle the warlock and his army on their own. Under the cover of a massive, magical storm, Mack himself had fought and defeated Auden on the beach of their small town, Willow Cove. Mack had even damaged the Horn of Power.

As the Changers soon discovered, though, Auden was down but not out. Mack and his friends clashed with Auden's henchmen as they sought out a magical artifact, Circe's Compass, which Auden could use to find younglings, or Changers who hadn't yet come of age. Auden needed the magic of five different younglings to mend the Horn of Power. Once the horn was repaired and Auden rounded up another army to march on Willow Cove, all hope seemed lost. But once again, the Changers pulled through, thanks in part to Fiona, who had learned a magical *selkie* song that stripped the evil warlock of his magic once and for all and destroyed the Horn of Power for good.

But perhaps even more shocking than their sudden victory a few months ago was a secret that had been revealed to them just before the battle: hundreds of years ago, Mack, Gabriella, Darren, and Fiona had been foretold to be the next leaders of Changer-kind. It wasn't chance that the four of them lived in the same small town of Willow Cove—a town that was also home to an important Changer base. It was also why the First Four took such an interest in Mack and his friends and why they were training them personally . . . and why Mack was so impatient for more information.

After a long three months of waiting, today—finally—the First Four planned to tell Mack and his friends more about the prophecy and what it meant for them.

Mack finished tidying up the living room and sought out his grandfather. He found Jiichan meditating in his office. Hearing Mack's footsteps, Jiichan opened his eyes and then smiled.

"Is everything ready, Makoto?" he asked.

"Almost," Mack said. "I just have to shovel the walk. . . ." In truth, something had been weighing heavily on Mack these last few months, ever since his last battle. Something *other* than the prophecy, but he wasn't sure if now was the best time to broach the subject with Jiichan again.

"I know the wait has been difficult for you," Jiichan began, sensing that Mack was holding something back. "But the time wasn't right to reveal the prophecy. You needed more training before beginning the next phase of your journey—"

"There's actually, um, something else that's been

bothering me, Jiichan," Mack cut in. "Remember how I saw a golden *kitsune* on the battlefield, with seven tails? Sefu said she used to be your student—"

Jiichan cut off Mack midquestion. "I've told you already that I will not discuss this, Makoto. I have lived a very long life, and not every memory I have is a happy one. There are some things that I simply choose not to dwell on."

Mack clenched his teeth. Jiichan could be so mysterious when he wanted to be. Mack knew that Changers lived much longer than humans—that Jiichan was at least a thousand years old but what could be so bad that his grandfather wouldn't even talk about it? Based on the First Four's reaction to the golden *kitsune*'s presence on the battlefield, he knew that she was important and possibly dangerous—too dangerous to be ignored.

"But—"

Jiichan interrupted again. "This is not a story I want to tell. Not now."

Any further argument was useless. Mack knew that he and Jiichan were alike in more than just their Changer ability—they could both be stubborn. With nothing else to say, Mack trudged to the kitchen and lit the fire under the teakettle before heading outside to shovel snow.

Will the time ever be right? Mack thought, seething.

More and more lately it had been bothering Mack how little the First Four revealed to him and his friends about the wider Changer world. It seemed like they divulged one little secret at a time, and even those secrets hid more secrets.

Secrets within secrets within secrets. I'm tired of being kept in the dark. Will they ever tell us the whole truth?

Just then a flash of light in the corner of Mack's eye caught his attention. He looked up and saw a streak of gold bolting across the tree-lined field in the distance.

Was that—? Mack thought as he started to walk forward to get a better look.

"Mack!" Gabriella called out a car window, jolting Mack from his thoughts. An SUV pulled into the drive then. Gabriella and Darren climbed out of the backseat, followed by Ms. Therian and Sefu from the front.

Mack looked into the distance again. He was almost sure . . . the golden *kitsune* . . .

But whatever he saw, it was gone.